The Walking River

An Ancient Coming of Age Fantasy

The Clan Chronicles - Book 2

by
J. S. Keim

Wild Quail Publishing

CHILDREN'S BOOKS BY J. S. KEIM

THE HIDDEN MOON SERIES:

The Hidden Moon – 1

Return to the Hidden Moon – 2

Trouble on the Hidden Moon – 3

THE CLAN CHRONICLES SERIES:

Kael's Quest – 1

The Walking River – 2

The Way Home – 3

OTHER BOOKS:

Kermit Greene's World

Trouble At The Winston Hotel… A Mouse Mystery

BOOKS BY JUDITH KEIM

THE HARTWELL WOMEN SERIES:

The Talking Tree – 1

Sweet Talk – 2

Straight Talk – 3

Baby Talk – 4

THE BEACH HOUSE HOTEL SERIES:

Breakfast at The Beach House Hotel – 1

Lunch at The Beach House Hotel – 2

Dinner at The Beach House Hotel – 3

Christmas at The Beach House Hotel – 4

Margaritas at The Beach House Hotel – 5

Dessert at The Beach House Hotel – 6

Coffee at The Beach House Hotel – 7

High Tea at The Beach House Hotel – 8

Nightcaps at The Beach House Hotel – 9

Bubbles at The Beach House Hotel – 10

Canapes at The Beach House Hotel – 11 (2025)

Sea Breezes at The Beach House Hotel – 12 (2026)

THE FAT FRIDAYS GROUP:

Fat Fridays – 1

Sassy Saturdays – 2

Secret Sundays – 3

THE SALTY KEY INN SERIES:

Finding Me – 1

Finding My Way – 2

Finding Love – 3

Finding Family – 4

The Salty Key Inn Series – Boxed Set

SEASHELL COTTAGE BOOKS:

A Christmas Star

Change of Heart

A Summer of Surprises

A Road Trip to Remember

The Beach Babes

THE CHANDLER HILL INN SERIES:

Going Home – 1

Coming Home – 2

Home at Last – 3

The Chandler Hill Inn Series – Boxed Set

THE DESERT SAGE INN SERIES:

The Desert Flowers – Rose – 1

The Desert Flowers – Lily – 2

The Desert Flowers – Willow – 3

The Desert Flowers – Mistletoe & Holly – 4

The Desert Sage Inn Series – Boxed Set

SOUL SISTERS AT CEDAR MOUNTAIN LODGE:

Christmas Sisters – Anthology

Christmas Kisses

Christmas Castles

Christmas Stories – Soul Sisters Anthology

Christmas Joy

THE SANDERLING COVE INN SERIES:

Waves of Hope – 1

Sandy Wishes – 2

Salty Kisses – 3

THE LILAC LAKE INN SERIES:

Love by Design – 1

Love Between the Lines – 2

Love Under the Stars – 3

LILAC LAKE BOOKS:

Love's Cure

Love's Home Run

Love's Bloom – (2025)

Love's Harvest – (2025)

Love's Match – (2026)

OTHER BOOKS:

The ABCs of Living With a Dachshund

Trouble At The Winston Hotel… A Mouse Mystery

Holiday Hopes

The Winning Tickets

For more information: **www.judithkeim.com**

PRAISE FOR J. S. KEIM'S BOOKS

THE HIDDEN MOON

"The Hidden Moon is a wonderful fantasy escape for middle grades. Jack, Collin and Danny come to know the people of Anron and are called to help them regain their freedom. The book is filled with shape-shifters, flying dragons and fun. I bought a copy for my grandson for Christmas and am hoping for more from this author."

"My granddaughter, age 9, loved this book, so it's not a book you should limit to just middle-grade kids. J. S. Keim has a great imagination that appeals to kids and she adds to that wonderful powers of description. This is a must read for both boys and girls and will definitely appeal to both. A great gift idea for hooking kids on reading and for inspiring their imaginations. They will love it!!!"

"A fun story filled with adventure and suspense. I liked that the author took time to really plan out the story and the characters, and you don't know what might happen next."

"Fun read, enjoyable for both adult and child; its high adventure for young space jockies.

Want to encourage your kids to read more? This is a good book for that purpose."

RETURN TO THE HIDDEN MOON

"There are heroes and villains . . . and bad-guy problems. But the kids get to sort it all out. Some of the "bad-guys" turn around, become "good-guys." That's a positive message for youngsters who read these books, and exactly what should be expected of an adventure story for young boys and girls."

"The magic that carries the two brothers and their friend off to another planet is every young person's dream. And all the creatures they encounter, who are mostly good, are described in such vivid detail. I could see them in my own imagination. Of course, there are the bad guys, but this is what keeps the book exciting."

KERMIT GREENE'S WORLD

"As I was reading this delightful book, I kept thinking how much I wished I'd had this when I was teaching. My gifted students loved doing a bird-eye and bug-eye sketch of the same item and this would have been great to read to go along with that. Also, as a former teacher, I

loved how math was interwoven in the story during a pivotal point in the plot. Great book for all kids and a fabulous addition to any teacher's classroom set of books."

"What a great book for children to transition into becoming readers. This is exciting, fun to read and delights the imagination!"

The Walking River

An Ancient Coming of Age Fantasy

The Clan Chronicles - Book 2

by
J. S. Keim

Wild Quail Publishing

The Walking River is a work of fiction. Names, characters, places, public or private institutions, corporations, towns, and incidents are the product of the author's imagination or are used fictitiously. Any resemblance to actual events, locales, or persons, living or dead, is coincidental.

Wild Quail Publishing

PO Box 171332

Boise, ID 83717-1332

ISBN# 978-1-965622-74-2

Dedication

To Children with Imaginations

CHAPTER ONE

The rising sun was hidden behind puffy, gray clouds that hung in the sky like gusts of smoke over a damp, slow-burning fire. Kael and Maida waved goodbye to the people of the Clan of the Big Hole and walked toward their next adventure. Gonter held onto Brota's leather collar to keep him from running ahead.

They climbed to the rim of the canyon, loaded furs on Brota, and shifted their heavy sacs on their backs. The clan had generously provided them with meat, fish, and herbs for the long walk ahead.

Tall, green grass waved in the light breeze that danced around them. The sweet smell of flowers filled the air. Traveling in the heat was different from making their way through the cold in the Land of Fire and Ice. They stayed under the shade of the trees and stopped often to take sips from their water bags.

At one stop, Maida set down her sacs, picked a handful of the colorful flowers, and wove them together to form a circle. Giggling, she placed the floral crown on top of her head and spun around.

Kael and Gonter jumped up and down, racing around her, enjoying the break from their travels. Gonter clapped his hands, and Brota jumped up on his hind legs, twirling in a dance of his own.

Suddenly, a strange humming noise filled the air, bringing them to a stop.

Kael turned around and froze. Thousands of tiny, red hopping insects descended upon them.

"Run!" shouted Gonter, sprinting ahead.

They grabbed their sacs and furs and dashed away from the dangerous cloud of insects. Still, they could not run fast enough.

Kael fought off the horrid creatures.

No larger than his thumb, black antennas extended from their tiny heads. Long, thin legs rubbed their tubular red bodies, producing the strange sound that rang in Kael's ears.

"Help!" he cried, swatting at them uselessly.

Maida let out a shriek. A mass of the insects had landed on the flowers in her hair and shredded them, eating everything until nothing was left.

Gonter waved his arms in the air, frantically brushing away the insects that circled him.

Brota howled and ran in circles, trying to outrun them. It was hopeless. As soon as one wave of the nasty creatures left, another came behind.

Kael knelt beside Maida and Gonter and pulled his furs around him.

The humming noise became shrill as the insects tried to reach them.

Shaking, Kael huddled on the ground. He could hear Brota whimpering and Maida sobbing. Gonter, who usually talked a lot, was silent.

Kael had no idea how long they had stayed on the ground when the humming noise ended as abruptly as it had started.

He peered out from under his furs and jumped to his feet.

The bodies of the flying red insects lay on top

of the green stubble that had once been tall grass. Most were still. Some made tiny, buzzing noises that soon ended.

Gonter and Maida emerged from their furs and stared at the scene.

"They have eaten everything in their path," said Maida. "See? No more grass, no more leaves on the trees."

"The bugs are either dead or dying," said Gonter, shaking bodies off his furs.

Kael brushed them out of his hair, wondering about living creatures that would eat themselves to death.

He stared at the destruction with shock. As Maida said, the trees that had held green leaves moments ago were now bare. The flowers that had added color and sweetness to the landscape were gone, their stalks nibbled to the ground. He wondered if this had something to do with Borlan's curse. In a fit of anger, Borlan, an older boy in his clan, had laid a curse on him that he would never live to become chief of their clan. It haunted his dreams and made him worried when things did not go well.

Maida made a sign of disgust and ran her fingers through her hair, brushing at it furiously to get them out of it. “I have never seen such a thing.”

“Nor have I,” Gonter said, brushing them off Brota’s coat. “We need to move away from this place before other strange things come.”

Kael picked up his sacs and brushed off dead insects.

“Ugh.” Maida dangled her sacs away from her and shook them hard.

Moving around the insects on the ground, they started walking again through the once-beautiful land. Not knowing what to expect, neither Brota nor Gonter raced ahead as usual. They walked solemnly beside Kael and Maida.

They followed the trail of destruction until they finally reached a cluster of trees that had some leaves remaining. A stream gurgled nearby.

Kael threw down his traveling sacs and furs and sprinted for the water. He let out a sigh of relief as the cool water washed over his skin. Dipping his head beneath the water’s surface, he shook the last of the insects out of his hair.

Then he floated on his back, gazing up at the darkening sky, wondering what other strange beings they might encounter. What would Ronoldo say about the red flying insects that had destroyed so much? The destruction reminded him of the Talloo's land, where a giant had captured men and forced them to cut down trees. He realized once more how important it was for all living creatures to get along.

A wave of stream water washed over his face. Kael sputtered and stood, his wet curls dripping water down his cheeks.

Gonter grinned at him mischievously.

Pushing aside deep thoughts, Kael threw himself at Gonter.

Amid much laughter, a water fight broke out. Maida joined them, splashing as hard as they. Brota pranced on the bank of the stream, howling at their play.

The time of play was a welcome relief for them all.

Later, resting on his furs, Kael studied the round circle of light in the dark sky, wondering at the mysteries of his world. He turned over on his side and thought of his family. When another had invaded his clan, his mother had sent him into the safety of the woods. When he emerged, he discovered he was the only one left, except for Ronoldo, the wise man in his clan, who was dying. How he longed to see his mother and sister and know that they were safe. He'd been searching for them ever since.

After several sunrises, they arrived at a lush, green field in the midst of a grove of trees. Flowers bobbed their colorful heads from between strands of green grass. Birds chirped and swooped above them. The whirring sound of their wings was gentle compared to that of the destructive insects they had left behind. Here, trees were large and plentiful. Their protective leaves provided a coolness that had been missing on the hot, dusty plain they had crossed.

A grin broke out on Gonter's dust-streaked face. "I hear the sound of rushing water."

Maida's eyes sparkled. "Could it be the Walking River?"

“Race you!” Gonter cried.

Brota barked and darted forward.

Kael took off after Gonter. Maida stayed at his heels. Their sacs bounced on their backs like playful pats as they leapt through the grass, laughing and shouting.

At the shore of a wide river, Gonter flung himself down on the ground, gasping for breath.

Kael and Maida caught up to him and sprawled out in the grass beside him, still laughing. Kael silently vowed he would beat Gonter in a race.

“We made it!” Gonter sat up and studied the area. “So? Where is the monster?”

All seemed normal. The water gurgled in the river as it flowed beyond them. Birds sang their songs. Bees buzzed and landed hungrily on flowers.

“How are we going to cross the river?” Maida said. “See the size of it.”

“It is too wide here,” agreed Kael. “We will have to hike along the riverbanks until we find a place where we can cross.”

They picked up their traveling sacs and furs

and began searching for a narrow spot. They were forced to stop at sundown, without success.

They made camp and settled down early, exhausted after their extended trek. Long after the others slept, Kael lay awake, worried. The monster might be the type that roamed in the dark. He lay still, listening. Then he heard it—a slap, slap, slapping noise.

"Gonter, wake up," Kael whispered, nudging him.

Gonter snorted, rolled over, and went back to sleep.

The strange sound continued.

"Maida," Kael hissed. "Hear that?"

Maida moaned and huddled under her furs.

Kael cupped a hand to his ear.

"Slap, slap, slap."

He glanced with disappointment at his sleeping companions and got to his feet. "Come, Brota. You and I will go see what is making that noise."

Kael took hold of the leather rope around Brota's neck and crept away. Not far from camp, he discovered a narrow path and followed it, ready to turn and run at a moment's notice.

The noise grew louder. Kael ducked into the bushes at the river's edge and grabbed hold of Brota's collar. Hardly daring to breathe, he peered through the thick green foliage.

The glow from the round circle of light in the sky shone down on large brown, furred animals swimming in the river. Kael watched, fascinated, as they pushed logs together with their tiny paws. Their faces skimmed the surface of the river. Their wide, flat tails slapped the water, creating the odd noises that had kept him awake.

A low rumble came from Brota's throat. Kael shushed him and took a firmer hold of the leather strip around his neck.

The animals in the river appeared not to have heard them. They continued to push logs together, forming some kind of walkway across the river.

So, that is it, Kael thought. That is how people cross the water. That is why it is called the Walking River.

Bursting with his secret, Kael started back to the camp, dragging Brota with him. After sunrise, when Gonter and Maida awoke, he would enjoy teasing them.

As Kael sat down on his furs, Brota's ears lifted, and he stared at the brush around them.

Kael stood and raised his spear.

A little girl approached him. "Food. I need food."

"Who are you? Where did you come from?" asked Kael. The girl was a few seasons younger than Maida. Her skin dress was dirty.

"I am Anen. My people crossed the bridge a couple of sunrises ago. I got left behind when I fell from the bridge. My new friend, Biva, saved me. He told me to hide until another group came, so I would not have to work for Gowlit."

Hearing their voices, Gonter and Maida awoke, automatically lifting their weapons.

"Hold on. This is Anen," Kael explained. She is hungry. She got left behind when her people crossed the river a few sunrises ago."

"Oh, you poor thing," said Maida. She approached the girl and hugged her.

Anen started to cry. "I need to find my family."

Hearing those words, so like his own wish, Kael promised himself that he would do everything that he could to return Anen to her people.

Anen sat by Maida as Maida prepared a meal of meat and berries.

As soon as she had finished eating, Anen leaned against Maida and fell into a deep sleep.

"She must be exhausted," murmured Maida, laying Anen down onto a fur and wrapping her in another.

"We are all tired," said Gonter. "We need to go to sleep. We have a lot to learn after sunrise."

Kael decided to wait to tell Gonter and Maida about the strange animals he had seen.

The sun was warm on Kael's face when he jumped up from his sleeping furs and joined Gonter and Maida at the fire. Anen was still sleeping.

"I know how to cross the river," he announced triumphantly.

Gonter gave him a playful punch on the arm. "Yes? How? Something you dreamed up in your sleep?"

Kael chuckled. “You will see.” Under Gonter’s suspicious stare, he laughed. “I will show you.” He chewed his dried meat and scooped the last of the mush from his wooden bowl.

“We will keep Anen with us. After we cross the river, we will help her find her people,” said Maida. “She is a sweet little girl.”

Kael and Gonter exchanged glances and nodded their agreement.

Anen awoke and went to Maida.

Maida fed her and then folded the furs Anen had used into a bundle. “You can keep them with you.”

Wide-eyed, Anen nodded. “Thank you.”

Eager to share his knowledge, Kael rose. “Ready? Follow me.”

Maida narrowed her eyes. “Where are we going?"

Kael grinned. “Leave your things here. You will see.”

Laughing to himself, he led them single file along the riverbank.

“Wait!” Gonter grabbed hold of Brota. “Listen.”

"What is it?" Maida edged closer to Kael, her eyes wide with fear.

Kael tried to keep a straight face. "They are probably animals with brown fur and funny tails." He turned to Anen and put a finger to his lips.

Maida frowned. "What are you up to, Kael?"

Kael could not hold back a laugh. "I heard those same sounds before falling asleep. I tried to get you and Gonter to go with me, but you would not wake up. Brota and I took a hike down here by ourselves. You will not believe what I saw."

They crept along the dirt trail beside the river and ducked behind the bushes where Kael had hidden.

"What are they?" whispered Gonter, peering through the leaves at the creatures in the water. "And what are they doing?"

"What funny tails they have," Maida said softly.

Anen remained quiet, as Kael had asked.

At that moment, the wide, flat tail of one of them slapped the water, sending droplets everywhere, splashing them.

"Ho! Ho! Ho!" came a voice from downriver. The water animals flew into a flurry of activity. Excited chatter broke out among them as they worked faster to push more logs together.

"Working hard, my brown furry friends?" The sound of the voice so close to them made Kael and his friends hide again.

"That is right," said the voice. "Get that bridge done. Word has it that three visitors were spotted during the night. Right, Owlit?"

Curiosity got the best of Kael. He lifted a leafy branch and peeked out.

A short man as round as the ripe red berries Kael liked stood nearby. Tiny feet and thin, short legs held the girth of his body aloft. He teetered back and forth as he paced along the river's edge. A Night Flier perched on his shoulder. The bird's head swiveled in all directions, allowing him to see out of large yellow eyes. It hooted, twisted its head around, and looked directly at Kael.

"Owlit, you have discovered our visitors," the odd man said. He patted the Night Flier on its head. "What took you this long?"

The man chuckled and pointed a finger directly at Kael. "You, there. Tell the other two to stand up and keep the wolf at bay. I know you are there."

Maida and Gonter slowly rose to their feet and stood beside Kael, wide-eyed.

"How did he know about us?" whispered Gonter.

"The Night Flier must have found us in the dark." Kael shivered at the thought of being spied upon.

Anen came out of the bushes and stood by Maida's side.

The round man approached them. "Well, well, well, who do we have here?" His eyes were as big as those of his pet and almost as yellow. Locks of brown hair curled around his small ears. The top of his large, round head was bald; his pink skin glistened in the sun. His long, narrow nose curved down to his lips.

If he had feathers, Kael thought with amusement, he would exactly resemble a round, pink Night Flier.

"There are four of you?" said the man. "What

happened? Where did you come from?" he asked Anen, who hid behind Maida.

"This is Anen. Her people crossed a few sunrises ago," said Gonter.

"Are the rest of you going to tell me, or do I have to guess who you are?"

Maida cleared her throat. "I am Maida, from the Land of Fire and Ice."

Yellow eyes turned to Gonter.

"I am Gonter," he dutifully stated, "from the Clan of the Mountain."

"You?" Yellow eyes focused on Kael.

Kael swallowed hard. There was something about this man he did not trust. "My name is Kael. I come from the Clan of the Forest."

"Four strangers. Good...good...good," said the round man.

Gonter glared at him. "And who are you?"

The man laughed. "Full of sass, are you? I am Gowlit." He pointed to the bird on his shoulder. "Owlit and Gowlit. We are a great pair."

Kael glanced at Gonter. He seemed as uneasy as Kael felt.

"Yes," Gowlit continued, his voice rising, "We

are quite a pair, though we like to have company. And we like to greet our visitors early on."

Gowlit waved them forward. "Come. Owlit and I are watching my fine friends build a walking bridge. That is how visitors walk across the river." He raised a finger in warning. "Only those who pay me well can walk across. And then, only if the bridge is completed."

"If they do not choose to cross here, how do they get to the other side?" Gonter asked.

Gowlit shrugged. "Who knows? I cannot say. It is a wide river."

Kael's stomach squeezed. There was not anything nice about the man who was smiling at them.

CHAPTER TWO

Gowlit patted his round stomach. "Say, say, say! I am hungry. Go back to your camp and get a meal started. Owlit and I will soon join you." He headed back down the river.

Kael stared at the man's back with dread.

Gonter shook his head. "Guess he thinks he can order us around."

"I do not like him," Maida said. "Why should we obey him?"

"If we want to find out more about crossing the river, we better do as he says." Kael sighed. "I do not like it any more than you do."

They reluctantly returned to their camp and set to work, rebuilding the fire. Maida pulled out the smoked meat that the Clan by the Big Hole had given them and went about making a stew. Anen watched her.

Gonter took a few practice whirls with his

sling. Kael sharpened his spear. At Maida's raised eyebrows, Kael nodded grimly. "We want to be ready in case we need them."

Gowlit and Owlit showed up as Maida declared the meal ready.

"Smells good," said Gowlit, smacking his lips. He sat on a log next to the fire and held out his hand. "Where is mine?"

Maida gave him a ferocious frown but handed him a bowl of stew.

Gowlit noisily slurped his meal and then leaned back and sighed. "Good, good, good."

"Do many people come here to cross the river?" Gonter asked.

Gowlit nodded.

"My clan usually travels to the Big Water by a different route. My grandfather dreamed we should travel there by way of the Walking River," said Maida.

"Then you must have interesting things to trade," said Gowlit, giving her a false smile.

"Is that how people get across?" Gonter asked.

Gowlit's eyes gleamed. "Indeed, indeed,

indeed. Many people travel here. Some are going to warmer places before their cold seasons. Some follow herds of animals for better hunting. They all have to depend on me to help them cross the river. That is how I survive."

Groaning loudly, Gowlit rose to his feet. "Well, well, well. I will be back at sundown. We can eat another meal then. Ready, Owlit?"

The large-eyed bird fluttered his wings and settled on Gowlit's left shoulder, and they strolled away.

After Gowlit left, Kael turned to Anen. "Tell us what you know about how your people crossed."

"And also, what happened to you?" Maida said.

"Everyone had to give Gowlit something of value," said Anen. "Then, my mother and

another woman were ordered to help tie the logs together. When all the logs were tied together, that man let our people across. As soon as I fell into the water, the bridge broke apart. Anen sighed. "I could not reach them, and they could not reach me. Biva, one of the animals, rescued me and tossed me onto shore. He told me to hide or Gowlit would make me work."

"I want to understand *why* those animals build bridges," said Kael.

"I want to see *how* they build bridges," Gonter said.

"And I want to know how long it takes," said Maida. "I do not like it here."

Gonter tied Brota to a tree, and the four of them traveled down the riverbank.

They had not gone far when one of the water animals blocked their path. A flat tail twice the size of his body dragged behind him as he pushed a huge log toward the river with his front paws.

"Humph," the animal said. "It is heavy."

Kael blinked in surprise, then remembered Ronoldo telling him that on his travels, he would meet animals who could talk. "Do you need help?"

"No, no," he answered with a firm shake of his head. "Then I, Biva, would not be busy. We like to keep busy, you see." He snorted and wheezed through large, white teeth that overlapped his lower jaw.

Biva continued to strain and stretch to get the log into the water, grunting and groaning with the effort. He waved away Kael's offer of help and then noticed Anen. "I see you are safe. That is good."

"Why are you working for Gowlit?" Gonter asked.

Biva's eyes widened. He gave his head a shake, as if only a fool would ask such a question.

"Yes, why do you do it?" Kael said.

"Gowlit has a lot of work for us, and we like it that way. We like to keep busy. We do not have to think about what we will do next; we do what he says. We are busy, we are."

Kael noticed a mound of sticks, mud, and grass sitting at the edge of the water farther down the river. "What is that?"

Biva stopped his work. "That is where I live."

He gave a final push to the log at his feet and followed it into the water.

"Wait!" cried Kael. "We want to find out more about Gowlit's bridges."

Biva gave them a last glance, disappeared

beneath the surface of the water, and swam away, pushing the log in front of him.

Kael stared at the mound along the riverbank and wondered how an animal could live there.

"I want to leave as soon as we can," said Maida, wrapping her arms around Anen and herself.

They stood on the banks of the river and watched Biva and his friends push logs together, forming a floating pathway that bobbed in the water.

Kael called to Biva and the others, but none of them paid any attention to him.

The sky darkened.

"We had better go back to the camp," Gonter said.

Back at the camp, Brota greeted them with a happy bark. Gonter untied him and laughed when Brota placed his paws on his shoulders and licked his cheeks.

While Gonter rebuilt the fire, Kael gathered enough wood to get them through the dark time. Maida took some of the cornmeal Serek's people had given them and mixed it with water in a bowl.

A short time later, Gowlit appeared and sat on a log, ready to be fed.

Kael and Gonter sat on the ground nearby.

“Who taught Biva and his friends to build a bridge?” asked Gonter.

“Who taught them? They always use logs to build things. It is the way they live,” said Gowlit.

“Is that all they do? Build bridges?” asked Maida.

“Well, well, well,” said Gowlit, shaking his head. “Another one full of questions, are you? They started building their houses. Then, I changed things.”

The hairs on the back of Kael’s neck stiffened. Gowlit sounded like the Talloo. Fidar had warned them about a different kind of monster. Was he talking about Gowlit?

Gonter shot him a troubled glance.

Gowlit laughed. “Why not? If I do not make things happen the way I want, I will not get my way. And I do not like it if that happens.” His smile evaporated. “What? What? What? You do not like what I tell you?" He pounded his chest. "It is *my* way or *no* way."

The bird on Gowlit's shoulder rose in the air with a flap of its wings and settled down once more.

"Even this feathered bird knows it is best if I handle things my way," said Gowlit. "Here in this part of the world, *I am* in charge, nobody else. Everyone works for me." He shifted on the log. "Well, well, well, where is our meal?"

Maida and Anen returned to the fire to check on the food.

"What is taking you so long?" Gowlit growled.

Maida and Anen served the food, and it grew quiet as they all ate.

Gowlit let out a loud belch and wiped his lips on his fur sleeve. "Say, say, say. That was tasty. Good of you to invite me to dinner. It was hospitable of you. Now I must go."

After Gowlit disappeared through the trees, Maida turned to the others.

"We have to get out of here. There must be a way we can cross the river faster. We are almost out of food, and we will have nothing to offer Gowlit. He might decide to keep us here to help him with his bridge."

"Biva is the key," said Kael. "We need to search the area."

"You are right. Biva is the head of them," said Anen.

"I will tie Brota up, to stop him from following us," said Gonter.

They made their way down the trail and crouched in the bushes lining the river. The light from the round circle in the dark sky washed the area with its brightness.

Biva and his friends were way out in the water, lining up logs to make a pathway. Gowlit stood at the water's edge, supervising.

"Good, good, good," he called. "Owlit has come back to me with news of more travelers heading this way. Hurry and get the bridge completed. Then, I will receive gifts from not one but two groups."

From their places of hiding, Kael, Gonter, Anen, and Maida silently watched the activity.

Sometime later, Gowlit raised his hands.

"Stop, stop, stop! That is enough for now." His body rolled and spun on his tiny feet as he walked away, down the riverbank.

The animals left in pairs, swimming down the river, until only Biva remained.

"I am going to try the bridge," said Kael, stepping out of the bushes.

Gonter nodded. "Maida and I will keep watch for you in case Gowlit returns."

"Take care," Maida said.

Heart pounding, Kael hurried to the edge of the water and put one foot on a few of the logs floating nearby. They rocked back and forth under his foot. Now he understood why they needed to be tied together.

Splash!

Kael landed in the cold river water with a gasp of surprise. He barely had time to take another gulp of fresh air before he was dragged down beneath the surface of the river. Twisting around, he saw brown fur and large white teeth.

Air! I need air! Kael drew his elbow forward and swung it back as hard as he could.

Bubbles came from the creature behind him.

The death grip on his shoulders loosened.

Kael kicked and spun upward through the water to the surface, sucking in fresh air in noisy gasps.

Biva glared at him. "What are you doing here? I told you to mind your own business."

"I was curious about the bridge," Kael said. "You almost drowned me."

"You have no business here at night." Biva shook a paw at him. "Where are those friends of yours? They are as nosy as you."

"I was testing the logs alone," Kael said truthfully, evading the question.

Biva shook his head. "You must leave things alone. I have an important job to do, trying to keep the logs together until they can be tied to one another. Gowlit's sister used to tie them. She finally quit. Went off with a group of visitors, she did."

"Why does Gowlit not do the work himself?"

Biva wheezed in and out in an odd little chuckle. "Gowlit? Work? The bridge would not hold him, anyway. Not when we are trying to put it together. We need someone in each traveling group to do the work, or nobody can leave."

"Do you never tire of all your work?" asked Kael.

Biva shook his head back and forth so fast that water flew from his face. "I am keeping busy, you know. It is the way of things around here."

"You work all the time," Kael said. "You should have rest, too."

"Well, you see, it is because... well, it is because..." Biva stopped and lifted his palms in the air. "I do not know...It is the way it is."

Kael shook his head. "You could play in the water with your friends or float on your back in the sun. You do not have to work all the time. Gowlit does not work at all."

Biva rubbed his chin. "Well, you see...it is because... well, let me think... perhaps a little rest would not hurt."

"I think you should start by helping us to leave as fast as possible," said Kael.

Biva sighed. "I am supposed to be busy all the time. That means work, not doing anything else."

A suspicion crept through Kael's mind. An ugly one. "Who told you this?"

"Why, uh…I suppose…well…Gowlit did. That is who," said Biva.

"I thought so," said Kael. "Tell me, was that how things were done before he came here to the Walking River?"

Biva suddenly appeared frightened. "I cannot talk to you about this. Gowlit would be angry with me. The others, too, are used to following his rules. It is the way of things."

Biva's brown furry body sank beneath the water.

As he swam away, his head was little more than a dark brown spot gliding along the surface of the river.

Kael watched him, thinking how mixed up things were at the Walking River. In his clan, it took hard work to simply stay alive. Still, time was also spent listening to stories of hunters, swimming in the river by his home, or playing games with some of the boys his age. What was wrong with having a little fun?

As Kael walked onto the riverbank, Gonter

and Maida ran to greet him. Anen stood watching them.

"Is Biva going to help us?" said Maida.

Kael shook his head. "I am not sure. Gowlit has told him and his friends they have to keep busy working all the time. He told them they cannot stop working. Biva is afraid to upset Gowlit."

Kael's stomach clenched. He was sure now that Gowlit was the kind of monster Fidar had talked about. Somehow, they had to meet this challenge. Like Maida had mentioned, they had nothing of value to give him.

CHAPTER THREE

In the early light, Gonter put a leather leash on Brota, and they all headed downriver to the bridge.

"Well, well, well, what do we have here?" Gowlit boomed, already on the job of watching the swimming animals push logs together. "Come, now. You two women need to set to work tying the logs together. And you young men need to hunt for food. When the bridge is done, we will have a celebration feast." Gowlit reached over to pat Brota.

Brota growled low in his throat.

"Go away, beast." Gowlit stalked off as best he could on his tiny legs.

Biva swam over to the edge of the river. "We have been busy, very busy. There is a mound of leather strips on the riverbank. You two women need to start right away if we are to get this bridge finished within a couple of sunrises."

Maida turned to Kael and Gunter. "A couple of sunrises? That is too long. Anen and I will work hard so we can escape at sundown."

Kael and Gonter nodded their agreement together.

"We will work something out," said Gonter. "We will have to move fast, or it will not work."

"Surprise is the key," Kael said. "You might have to pretend the work is not done while completing enough to allow us to escape."

Maida and Anen went to work tying the logs together. As soon as they got one set of logs done, they moved to the next. It was slow, tedious, backbreaking work.

While the girls were still working, Gonter stepped onto the bridge. Brota pulled back so hard that the leather strip around his neck broke.

"Come, boy," said Gonter, tugging on the fur around Brota's neck. "It is all right. Come with me."

No matter how much Gonter coaxed, Brota

refused to get on the logs.

"If he sees all of us on the bridge at sunrise, he might follow," said Kael, hoping it was true. The wolf had never liked water. Especially after being caught in the flood in the Talloo's land.

Kael approached Maida, kneeling on the logs in the middle of the river. Biva and his friends held the logs in place with their broad tails while she wound strips of leather around one log, tying it to the next one, knotting the leather carefully.

He knelt down beside Maida. "We leave at sunrise," he whispered.

Biva shook a furry fist at Kael. "Do not get in the way. The women need to keep busy. We have work to do."

Kael made his way back across the completed portion of the floating bridge.

Gonter watched from the riverbank, Brota at his side.

When Kael approached him, Gonter shook his head. "Brota will not come onto the bridge. I do not know what to do with him."

Kael exchanged a worried look with Gonter. They had to make their escape at sunrise and take Brota and Anen with them.

At sundown, Gowlit appeared at the fire.

Brota backed away when Gowlit reached down to pat him and began to growl. On Gowlit's shoulder, Owlit fluttered his wings and stared at the wolf with round, yellow eyes.

"What do we have for dinner? Fresh meat?" Gowlit took a seat on a wide log by the fire and rubbed his hands together in anticipation. "After our meal, we will do some trading. That is, if all of you want to cross the river." Gowlit licked his lips. "What are you giving me to eat?"

Maida held out a wooden bowl to him. "I have mixed cornmeal, chunks of Hopper meat, and wild berries, like the women of the Clan by the Big Hole showed me."

Gowlit took the bowl with a smile. "Good, good, good."

After he had finished his third bowl of food, Gowlit stood and burped loudly. "Now, we need to talk about trading. I travel up and down the river, trading with others who come to find a crossing."

“We have nothing but food to trade, and not much of that,” Kael said.

“Well, well, well, hard to believe you have nothing of value.” Gowlit glanced at their skin travel sacs. His eyes glowed with greed. “In addition to food, I am usually given weapons and other gifts of interest. You must have something to show me.”

Gonter shook his head. “We have no treasures. Our weapons are nothing more than leather strips and one spear that we cannot give up.”

The gleam in Gowlit’s eyes faded. His brow furrowed into disappointed lines. “I want food and weapons to trade.”

“Like Gonter said, we have nothing that would be of value to you,” Kael said, wishing he had kept his spear at his side. Gowlit’s expression was turning nasty.

“Only a few precious stones and paintings,” Maida said, trying not to smile at her white lie.

Gowlit shrugged. “If you cannot do better than that, I may have to keep you here to help for a while, until the next group comes. You can hunt for food for me. "

He left the campsite, patting his round stomach.

"Do you think Gowlit fell for our trap?" asked Maida.

"We had better hope so, or we are in trouble."

Fingers of light flexed in the dark sky. Dawn was near.

Kael lay on his sleeping furs, waiting to see if the trap they had set for Gowlit would work.

Brota raised his head and perked his ears. Gonter laid a hand across Brota's snout, silencing him.

Maida and Anen lay motionless near him, but Kael knew they, too, were wide awake, ready to take action.

Gowlit appeared, sneaking into the campsite on his tiny feet, heading for the carrying sacs they had placed together near the fire. The idea of precious stones and paintings was too enticing for him.

Gowlit snatched up a carrying bag and sat on a log, pawing through it.

Gonter let go of Brota.

The wolf raced toward Gowlit, growling.

Gowlit jumped to his feet. “Stop, stop, stop!” He dropped the bag and held his hands out in front of him. “Get this beast away from me. I have taken nothing.”

The four of them formed a circle around him.

“You may not have stolen anything,” Gonter said, “but you intended to do just that. We are young, but we know about people like you.” He turned to the others. “Now?”

“What, what, what!” cried Gowlit. “What are you going to do?”

Kael shooed the Night Flier off Gowlit’s shoulder. “Fly away! The dark time is almost over.”

The bird took off with a flap of its wings. A soft hoot streamed like a song behind him.

Maida handed Kael leather strips. As Gonter, Brota, and Anen stood guard, they tied Gowlit’s hands together.

“Move over there,” said Gonter, “by that tree.” He prodded Gowlit with a stick.

"No, no, no!" Gowlit said.

Brota approached him, snarling.

"Yes, yes, yes."

Gonter guided Gowlit to the tree and pushed him down to the ground. Gowlit sat wide-eyed as they bound his feet together, winding strips around and around them, much like how Maida and Anen tied the logs of the bridge. Then, they tied him to the tree.

"It is only right that we are tying you up after all the work you have made others do, tying logs together, then stealing from them," Kael said.

"No, no, no..." Gowlit began.

Kael ignored his sputtering and walked away to gather his things. He hoped the rest of their plan would work as well.

"All right," said Gonter.

Kael hurried away from the campsite with Maida, Anen, and Gonter.

At the water's edge, they stood together.

Biva's head rose from the water. "What are you doing here?"

"We are escaping, and we need your help," said Maida.

"I work for Gowlit," Biva said stubbornly.

"You do not have to work for anyone." Kael desperately tried to think of words that would change Biva's mind. "You can think for yourself. And staying busy can sometimes mean having rests, too. You did not want to talk about it earlier. Now we must. We need your help."

"But...well...where is Gowlit?"

"Gowlit is back at the campsite," Kael explained. "We tied him up. You can untie him in a while. He will be fine." Kael snorted in disgust. "He will probably be ready to eat someone else's food or steal their things."

Biva let out a sigh that echoed off the logs surrounding them. "I cannot ... you see ... it is the way we do things here..."

Kael studied Biva. "It is sometimes wise to make changes, especially if it helps others."

"I want to go home, Biva." Anen's eyes filled with tears.

The expression on Biva's face turned tender. "Well, ... I suppose... what will Gowlit say?"

"Help us," said Kael.

"It is all right to have some rests?" Biva

studied Kael with something like hope.

Kael and the others nodded.

Cautiously, they stepped onto the bridge that was almost complete.

The other animals formed a group behind Biva.

"What are you doing?" one of them asked Biva. "You are supposed to protect the bridge."

"I am making a change to our routine," said Biva with a fierceness that sent a thrill through Kael. "Now, we need to get busy holding logs together for these travelers."

Anen leaned over and kissed the top of Biva's head. "Thank you for saving me."

"Well...I...well...I am going to miss you," he said, looking sad.

"No, no, no!" came a cry from the edge of the river.

Gowlit ran along the riverbank and onto the bridge, rocking it dangerously as he hurried toward them, one tiny foot after the other.

Kael's jaw dropped. "How did he get free?"

"Probably Owlit," said Maida. "He has a sharp beak."

Brota was right behind Gowlit, nipping at his heels. Owlit flew around in circles above GowlIt is head.

"Good for you, Brota. Here, boy," cried Gonter.

"Hurry!" said Maida. "Grab your things. The end of the bridge is not finished. It will never hold Gowlit, but we can escape if Biva and his friends help us."

Kael picked up his sacs and furs and raced after Maida and Anen, running hand in hand in front of him.

"If we keep moving, Brota will keep coming," said Gonter.

Balancing on the logs with full hands was no easy task. Kael managed to keep upright. Freedom was steps away.

Biva swam alongside the bridge. "I want to watch this," he said, snorting with laughter. "This is too much ... too much ... to pass up."

"Stop!" screeched Anen, holding up her hands.

Ahead of them lay loose logs floating in the water.

"Biva, help us," she cried.

Biva reached up and touched the spot where Anen had kissed him. "Wait ... no ... I see... Well, for you ... Let me get the others..."

He let out a whistle. "Everyone, come here!"

The brown furry animals swam over and pushed the logs together, holding them in place with their flat tails.

Anen and Maida ran forward.

Kael and Gonter took a giant leap together.

"We made it!" cried Kael, landing on solid ground. "Biva! The logs. Release them."

Biva started to shake his head, and then he shrugged. Glee filled his furry face. He signaled for his friends to move away.

The logs separated as Gowlit's feet hit them. For a brief moment, he stood suspended in air, his face a mask of round surprise. Then his body entered the water with a loud splash. He kicked and splashed as the river carried him downstream like a round, red berry bobbing along the surface.

Brota stood at the end of the tied bridge, howling.

“Come, boy,” said Gonter.

Brota hesitated, then jumped into the water and swam to Gonter’s outstretched hands.

Kael turned to Biva. “Thank you. You saved our lives.”

Biva smiled and lay in the water, floating on his back. “I like doing this,” he murmured and closed his eyes.

Kael grinned and headed away from the Walking River.

“Home,” said Anen. “I want to go home.”

"We are going to help you find your clan," said Gonter, patting her on the shoulder.

The thoughts of his family sent waves of homesickness through Kael. It had been many sunrises since he had seen his mother and sister, Rarey.

“How will we find Anen’s family?” Gonter said quietly so the little girl, walking ahead, would not hear. “It is a great distance to the Big Water.”

Kael shook his head and glanced at the girl traveling alongside Maida. She was little but strong. Strong enough, he hoped to keep up with them as they met dangerous challenges ahead.

CHAPTER FIVE

At sundown, they stopped and set up camp.

They formed a routine with each person contributing. Kael and Anen made the roof structures out of twigs and leaves to hang between trees, protecting them. Gonter gathered wood and tended to the fire. Maida took care of feeding them.

After eating, they lay down on their furs, huddling close together for protection.

The quiet was broken by a sudden rustling of leaves in the trees.

"What's *that*?" Anen's voice shook with fear, and she sat up, staring around her.

Out of the darkness came a muted "hoot".

Kael laughed. "It is only a Night Flier."

"Night Fliers are supposed to bring good fortune," said Maida, sitting up on her soft furs.

The bird swooped down and glided to a

landing near Anen. She shrieked and ducked under her furs.

Brota barked and rose to attack.

"Wait!" said Gonter, holding onto Brota. "It is Owlit. I recognize the little collar around his neck."

The large-eyed bird swiveled its head and stared at Gonter as if to say, "Who-o-o-o else?"

Kael grinned. "He must have decided Gowlit's way of doing things was not what he wanted, after all."

Anen stuck her head out from beneath her furs. Owlit hopped over to her sleeping place, inspected it, and flew up into a branch nearby.

"There," said Gonter. "It is all right."

Kael and the others settled back on their furs. With the bird guarding them from on high, they soon fell asleep.

At sunrise, they prepared to leave. Owlit flapped his wings and swooped down on Anen's shoulder. The sight of the large bird atop little Anen made them all laugh.

"Is he too heavy? Should I chase him away?"

asked Kael, still chuckling.

Anen stood to her full height. “No. I like him sitting there. It reminds me of my time at the Walking River. He is free now, too.”

They traveled through the woods, following Anen’s suggestion of where to go.

From time to time, Owlit flew away and soon came back to settle on Anen's shoulder, keeping watch over her.

It was dark when they came to a halt. They set up sleeping places and hung strips of meat over the fire to cook.

“We are running out of meat,” said Kael. He took a last bite of his meal and wiped his greasy hands on nearby leaves.

“Let’s keep an eye out for animals as we walk,” said Gonter. “Even if it means we do not travel as fast.”

Maida gave them a teasing smile. “I bet I can catch an animal before either of you boys do.”

Warming to the challenge, Kael grinned at Gonter.

It became a game to see who could see the first animal and catch it. They stopped often to search through thick underbrush or to listen to the sounds of animals in the woods.

They had walked some distance when Owlit flapped his wings and rose from Anen's shoulder with a screech that sent shivers down Kael's spine.

They huddled together with raised weapons. Owlit's alarm could mean anything.

"What is it?" Anen asked in a shaky voice.

Kael smelled something foul. Something rotten. It brought back a memory he had tried to chase from his dreams.

"Watch out!" he cried, lifting his spear. "It is a Gouger."

A long snout, flanked by sharp curling horns, a wide head, barged through the thick-leaved bushes in front of them. Then, a large, dark, hairy body followed, atop four skinny legs with tiny sharp hooves.

Kael's heart pounded so hard he could barely breathe.

Brota lunged toward the beast, nipping at its feet, slowing its charge. The vicious animal swerved away from Brota and headed in Anen's direction.

Anen screamed and ran. She tripped on a tree root, going down with another scream of terror.

Adrenaline pumped through Kael. He ran towards the Gouger, shouting and waving his arms at the Gouger's face.

Maida ran up behind the Gouger and jabbed it in the flanks with the long stick she had used for walking.

As the three of them shouted and poked at him, the Gouger halted in confusion.

Its talons stretched out for the kill, Owlit swooped down and landed on the Gouger's head.

A high-pitched squeal from the Gouger tore at Kael's eardrums. The beast turned in circles, struggling to shake Owlit off its head. Blood dripped down its furry face.

Anen scrambled to her feet and raced to Maida's side. "Owlit saved me. You all saved me."

Fascinated and horrified at the same time, Kael watched the fierce battle continue. Owlit had been a sleepy, quiet Night Flier on Anen's shoulder. Now, he was a screeching, deadly creature, intent on bringing down his prey, ripping the flesh around the eyes of the beast.

Roaring, the Gouger fell, his body wounded and bleeding. With a triumphant screech, Owlit lifted off the beast and flew up to a branch above them.

Gonter took the first shot at the Gouger with his sling. The stone flew through the air like the kiss of death and landed on the beast's face right between his wounded eyes. It fell over on the ground with a heavy thud.

Kael let fly his spear, piercing the beast's chest.

Maida twirled her sling. The stone landed on the Gouger's snout with a bone-cracking sound.

Breathing heavily, they waited and finally crept closer.

"I have never seen such an ugly, smelly beast," said Maida, holding her nose.

"Once before, I have killed a Gouger," said Kael. "That is why I was chosen to go into the forest with the hunters from my clan."

"Our hunters like the skin of Gougers," said Anen, staring at the dead beast with wide eyes.

"And we eat their meat. It is tasty."

"We had better take the meat we need and move on before other beasts come for their share," Kael said.

They worked fast to remove the fur skin from the Gouger. Maida showed Kael how to carve meat from its ribs with the sharp bone knife her grandfather had made her. They rolled up chunks of meat in the fur of the Gouger and tossed some leftovers to Brota.

"Are we ready to go?" Gonter asked, wiping his brow.

The heavier loads of meat made their travel slower and more dangerous.

The sun was still high in the sky when Gonter stopped them. "We had better take care of this raw meat. If not, other animals will smell it and come after us."

They found a clearing in the forest and hunted for wide, hollow pieces of wood. Using them to scoop out dirt, they dug a large, shallow hole. Then they loaded up the hole with kindling, made a fire, and stacked larger chunks of wood nearby.

With her sharp knife, Maida began cutting the meat into slices.

While they were waiting for the fire to burn down, Kael and Gonter set to work on a smoking rack. They placed thin green branches on the ground in a grid pattern. Maida and Anen used flexible vines to tie them together.

The boys dragged a large log and a weathered tree stump over to the fire. They placed them on opposite sides of the pit.

"There. Now we are ready for the rack," said Kael.

He and Gonter lifted the rack, set one end on the ground beside the fire, and rested the far corners of it on the log and stump. It formed a slope for cooking the meat above the hot, glowing coals.

"The hunters in my clan prepare meat this way so it will not spoil while they travel," said Gonter.

Maida nodded. "In the Land of Fire and Ice, we store meat by packing it in ice. When we travel to the Big Water, we must dry and preserve the meat like this."

Hungry, Brota paced back and forth. In a tree above them, Owlit fanned his wings, causing them to glance at the thick woods with worry.

As soon as the last strip of meat came off the rack, they built a roaring fire, bright enough and hot enough to keep away hungry predators.

They sat around the fire and ate as much as they could.

Warm grease from the meat slid down Kael's chin as he bit into another tender piece.

After he had had his fill, Kael lay atop his furs and let out a sigh of contentment. Their moments of terror when fighting the Gouger had ended in a good way. Brota had fought to save them, and Owlit had flown to their rescue. Perhaps, man and beast were meant to live in harmony with each other, like the Man of the Mountain had told them. It was something he would think about.

At sunrise, they traveled through the deep, dark forest and entered a welcoming place where tall pines stood with white-barked trees.

They had walked for a while when Brota

stopped and growled. The fur on his back rose.

Kael lifted his spear.

Gonter jumped back and pointed to a huge shape peering at them from between thick pine branches.

Kael froze. A huge, black Growler stared at them, its sharp, white teeth gleaming wickedly from its open mouth. His heart pounded in loud thumps. He gripped his spear tightly. A Growler was the beast he most feared. A Growler had killed his father.

“Something is strange,” Gonter said softly. “The Growler has not moved or shown any sign of life." He let go of Brota, who moved forward cautiously.

They all followed him.

One frightening face, then another, appeared below that of the Growler.

Kael stared in awe.

“It is a huge tree, with carvings.” Maida reached out and touched the surface. “Each face is painted with bright colors. I wish our friend Serek were here to see it. I wonder if he has ever seen anything like this.”

“Growlers scare me.” Anen drew closer to Kael.

“This is not real,” said Gonter. “See the Night Flier, Anen? It is like Owlit.”

Owlit fluttered his wings and settled back down on Anen’s shoulder.

Several hunters broke through the trees and surrounded them.

“Who are you?” asked a short, wide man, stepping forward. One hand was raised in a gesture of peace, while the other gripped a spear as tall as he was. Dark, straight hair was held back from his face by a wide band of leather placed around his head. Animal skins covered his torso.

“This little girl,” grunted another man. “She carries a sacred Night Flier. It is a sign.”

The hunters began talking among themselves, pointing at Anen and Owlit. The man who had first spoken turned to them.

“I am Winno, chief of the Clan of Fierce Faces. Our people would be honored if you would spend some time with us. We have been expecting a sign of good fortune. The Night Flier and the little girl have given it to us."

Kael exchanged glances with Gonter and Maida and nodded. "The girl is called Anen. We will be honored to spend time with you. We are on our way to the Big Water and have grown tired of walking."

"We had already planned a feast. Now, it shall be in honor of Anen," said Winno. "Come, we will lead you to our village." He shot a worried glance at Brota. "Is it safe to have this gray Howler with us?"

Gonter patted Brota on the head. "He will not hurt you. He is my pet. I have had him since he was a baby."

Winno nodded. "All right. We will allow him among us." He shook a finger at Gonter. "You must keep a careful watch over him. Come."

Curious to see how this clan lived, Kael picked up his belongings and followed the men through a thick grove of trees into a wide clearing.

A huge log structure stood in the center.

Gonter grinned. "They live in one big house like my clan."

“Yes, and there's another carved tree by the door,” said Maida.

“I want to find out how they make those trees like that," said Gonter, "so my people can make them, too.”

A group gathered around them, pointing to Anen and Owlit and murmuring to themselves.

“Listen, my people, and gather closer,” said Winno. “Here is the sign of good fortune we have been waiting for. We will prepare a feast in honor of the girl called Anen and her Night Flier.”

He turned to Kael. “Tell us about yourselves.”

Kael drew himself up and faced the sea of eager, curious faces. “I am Kael, from the Clan of the Forest. My friends and I are traveling the world. I am searching for my mother and sister. They were taken captive by another clan. I also want to learn about our world.”

“And I am Gonter,” he said. “I come from the Clan of the Mountain. It is our mission to share what we learn with others.”

“And I come from the Land of Fire and Ice,” said Maida. “I have been trained to hunt and fish, to prepare for this journey. We found Anen at the Walking River. She fell in the water and was left behind when her clan crossed the river."

"They rescued me," said Anen, her eyes shiny. She took Maida's hand.

An old woman stepped forward. Her back was stooped, her face wrinkled and aged, but her dark eyes gleamed with life as her gaze swept over them and came to rest on Anen.

"My name is Tesi. I have good news for you, Anen. Your people left here not long ago. They stayed with us for as long as they could, searching for you. Then, they had no choice but to move on."

"My mother was here?" Anen's face lit up with joy.

"I will send a runner after her," said Winno. "We have much to celebrate."

"Come with me, child," said Tesi. "We need to talk." She placed a hand on Maida's shoulder. "You, too."

"Let the women greet the young girls," said Winno. "We men want to learn more about your travels." He eyed the sling hanging around

Gonter's waist.

Gonter unwound it and held it up. "Have you ever seen a sling?"

Winno shook his head. "What do you do with it?"

"It can be used for hunting or as a weapon against enemies."

"A weapon?" Winno's face registered his disbelief. "Our clan makes a strong spear, stronger than all the others. We will show you how if you demonstrate your sling."

Kael and Gonter led the hunters over to a flat area at the edge of the village. Kael marked the center of a large tree with a circle of dark brown dirt. "Gonter will hit this spot from a long distance away."

Gonter loaded a stone into the leather fold at the end of his sling and motioned the men aside.

Chatting with excitement, the hunters gathered in a group next to Kael.

Gonter swung the leather strip around and around above his head, letting the stone fly at exactly the right moment. It landed in the center of the circle on the tree trunk with a deep-sounding thud.

"Ah-h-h-h," said Winno, nodding his head with admiration. "You can bring down an animal from a distance. That is the purpose?"

"Yes. With a large animal, it takes more than one sling. You need the use of a spear or two," Gonter explained. "You can bring down a smaller animal with one stone if you hit them in the right spot."

Winno held out his spear. "Now that you have shown us your sling, I will show you our new spears." He held out a long, straight tree branch.

Kael fingered the wood, noting how smooth it was.

"We recently designed a new style of spear," Winno explained. "It was something Tesi dreamed about. See how the wood is split at the end? We insert a sharp stone and wrap it with strips of animal hide. The stone makes the spear stronger and sharper than the ones we once used with carved, pointed ends. The spears fly faster and truer with the added weight."

"We used long, wooden spears to save captive

men in a place far from here," said Kael, thinking of the Fliers at the Talloo's land. "It would have been much easier using your new spears."

"Can we watch you make one so we can show the people of our clans?" Gonter asked.

"Yes," said Winno. "Tell us about your people. We want to learn new things, too. Come. Let us go to our meeting place."

They walked from the open field to the edge of the woods. There, among the trees, stood a wooden structure, the likes of which Kael had never seen. A rectangular roof was held up by four poles, one at each corner. The back wall was made of logs stacked on top of one another.

"The wall keeps out the cold wind. The open sides keep us cool in the warm times," Winno explained.

Seated on logs inside the structure, Kael and Gonter told the others about their clans.

"You said your father was a great hunter," one of the men said to Kael. "He approves of your traveling the world for your people?"

Kael blinked rapidly against the tears that sprang to his eyes. "My father died fighting a

Growler. He fought it alone so that others could escape." Kael touched the leather string that hung around his neck. "This Growler's claw is a reminder of his courage."

"I sense you also have great courage," came a woman's voice.

Kael whipped around.

Tesi walked into the meeting place, followed by Maida and Anen. She sat down with the men, who had formed a circle around Kael and Gonter.

"It is good that you and your friends seek wisdom," she told Kael. "People of all clans need to learn from one another if we are to survive in this world."

Goose pimples raced up and down Kael's body. Tesi sounded like Ronoldo. Did each clan have one special person who knew so much more than the others?

Winno asked Maida to tell the group about her clan. Maida spoke about her grandfather and how her people traveled to the Big Water before the cold time began in the Land of Fire and Ice.

Winno stood. "It is a time of celebration

when clans come together. We have much to share."

The group began to disperse.

"Come with me," said Tesi to the boys. "I have a place for you in the Big House."

Another clan, another home, thought Kael. He had come a great distance since he was left alone to fend for himself after his clan was raided.

CHAPTER SIX

Kael paused inside the doorway of the log house and allowed his eyes to get accustomed to the dimness. A fire blazed in the center of the huge space. Unlike Gonter's home, where stones marked each family's space, the interior walls were lined with sleeping places, one atop the other.

"Your homes are not like this?" Tesi gave them a knowing smile.

Kael shook his head. "Mine is small and made of mud and sticks. My mother, sister, and I are the only ones who lived there after my father was killed."

"My home is big like this and made of logs, but we do not have wooden sleeping places built into the walls," said Gonter. "We sleep on the ground."

"We build sleeping places, so we have room

to store our things," explained Tesi. "During our long rainy wet season, we need to be able to spread out inside. The children, especially, need space to play, and our women need room to spread furs so they can sew them together."

Tesi led them over to a section where sleeping places had no furs. "There is space here for your things," she said, indicating an area beneath the lowest bunk. "Choose which place you want to use. Maida and Anen have already done so, on the opposite side of the building with me."

Gonter chose the space closest to the ground so Brota could sleep by him. Kael selected the place above him.

"Come," said Tesi. "We will eat a simple meal. Our celebration will begin at the next sunrise, and then we will eat our fill."

"We have meat to share," Kael offered.

She smiled. "Save it for our celebration."

Though there were no formal lines dividing them, different families sat in clusters inside the log building, eating and talking. Kael, Gonter, and the girls sat with Tesi.

After the meal of fish and grain, Tesi rose. "Go to your sleeping places. We all awaken with the sun."

One by one, families began preparing for the dark time. Children were placed in sleeping places high above the ground. The smallest were protected from falling out by wide strips of skin tied onto the wooden frames.

"Why do the parents sleep closest to the ground?" Kael asked Tesi.

"The men of the clan must be ready to defend their families from wandering animals, if necessary. They keep their spears below their sleeping places, ready to fight. Growlers are plentiful here. Sometimes they break through the fur-covered entrance."

"Growlers?" Blood ran cold inside Kael. The memory of his father's death flashed in his mind. Of all the dangerous creatures in the world, a Growler was what Kael feared most.

He climbed into his sleeping place, feeling as if he were perched on a branch of a large pine tree. His sleeping place at home was simply furs spread on the ground inside his hut. The strangeness of it all and the worry about Growlers kept him tossing and turning.

At dawn, Kael arose, stretched, and jumped down from his sleeping place. Frightened to be outside alone, he shook Gonter awake. Together, they went into the cool, damp outdoors.

Kael blinked with surprise at all the activity. Women were lugging baskets of fish from the nearby river. A group of men chatted as they hauled a huge log into the open grassy area outside the building.

Kael finished his rituals and hurried over to them. “What are you doing?”

One of the men turned to him with a smile. “This log will become the story pole for our celebration. We will carve it and paint it to remember the time you were here.”

“Can we watch?” Gonter asked.

“Yes,” answered the man. “It is Doran you will want to watch, not me. Doran is the carver in our clan. Go and eat now. He will begin soon.”

Kael and Gonter raced back inside the log house.

“The carver is going to tell a story in wood,”

Kael told Maida, and eagerly accepted a bowl of mush from Tesi.

“We need to hurry,” Gonter said, gulping down a big bite of his meal.

Maida grinned and set down her empty wooden bowl. “I want to see this.”

As soon as they had finished eating, Kael and Gonter followed Maida and Anen outside. A grown man, the size of a child, approached them. “Ah, I see you are curious about my carvings.” He waved his short arms. “I need a symbol to help tell your story.” He pointed to Brota. “This gray Howler is most unusual. We have never seen one like him. Help me up onto the log. As you can see, I am too short to reach from one side to the other. I will sit on top of the log and begin there.”

Anen and the children of the clan gathered around. Some adults stood on the sidelines.

“What will it be, Doran?” called out one of the children.

“You must wait,” he answered, and closed his eyes in concentration. Then he began carving. The sharp stone he held in his hand flashed in the sunlight. Chips of wood flew in all directions. Within a short time, two eyes could be seen above a furry nose. Then two pointy ears perked above the eyes. The suggestion of a furry neck appeared next.

A smile spread across Kael's face. "It is Brota."

"It is perfect." Gonter patted Brota on the head. "Now everyone will remember him."

"Who will paint it?" asked Maida.

"I will," said a tall man who had been observing the carving. "When Doran tells me, I will use colors to finish decorating the pole."

Doran nodded. "Pica and I have worked together for a long time. He will not begin his work until I am done with mine. Now, continue with your story."

"On our way here from the Walking River, we fought a Gouger," said Gonter. "We are going to share that meat with you at the feast."

Doran cupped his face in his hands and closed his eyes. Soon, he sat up straight and his hands began their work—cutting, chipping, carving.

The scary face of a Gouger, complete with long horns, appeared on the wood.

Kael exchanged glances with Gonter. It seemed real. Too real. Kael gave Anen a pat on the back. Without Owlit's help, the Gouger could have killed her.

When Doran took a break, Chief Winno came up to them. "Are you ready to teach our men how to use slings?"

Gonter nodded. "Maida knows how, too."

Winno frowned. "A girl doing such a thing?"

"Yes," said Tesi, joining them. "Maida's grandfather was told in a dream to teach her those things so she could go out into the world."

"We can teach more people if she helps," said Kael quietly, defending her. "She is a skilled hunter."

Winno shrugged and turned away.

"So be it," said Tesi. "The three of you can show our hunters the way you use your slings. I will stay with Anen. Her mother should be here soon."

After Kael, Gonter, and Maida demonstrated how to use slings, they were taken to a place in the woods where a number of young saplings grew.

"Pick a tiny tree," said Winno. "We will teach you how to make a spear as strong as our best."

Kael selected the tree with the straightest trunk he could find. One of Winno's men cut it down with one swipe of a stone hatchet, trimmed off all the branches, and evened off the narrow top.

The hunter sliced a slot in the top of the pole, only wide enough to place a thin, pointed stone inside. Then he wrapped strips of animal hide around and around the slot, securing the stone.

Winno held it up for Kael's inspection. "It is important to tie the stone inside the sapling carefully, or else it will slip." He gave the spear to Kael. "Hunt well."

"You also," said Kael politely, handing Winno one of his extra slings.

Kael held his new spear in his hands, testing its balance. He smiled. It was easier to handle than his old one.

"Time to go back to the others," Winno announced. "I hear the voices of strangers."

Kael, Maida, and Gonter followed Winno to the entrance of the log house. Anen stood with Tesi and two adult strangers.

Anen pointed to Kael and waved to Gonter and Maida. “Mother, they are the ones who saved me.”

Anen’s mother approached. Without saying a word, she wrapped her arms around Kael.

His cheeks turned hot. He thought of his own mother, and a stab of homesickness hit him in his belly.

Anen’s mother moved from Kael to Gonter and Maida, greeting them with warm hugs. Then she stood back, beaming at them.

“I am Anen’s mother, Rutti. Thank you for saving my daughter from a cruel, selfish man like Gowlit. She told me what you did for her.”

Maida smiled. “Biva, one of the animals that lives there, found her alone and saved her from drowning.”

Rutti shook her head sadly. “It was heartbreaking. We tried to cross the river upstream, but it was raining hard, and the river rose up unexpectedly. Anen slipped out of my grip. I tried to go after her, and she was gone." Tears wet Rutti's face. She pulled Anen to her side.

A tall man came up behind Rutti and placed his hand on her shaking shoulders. "I am Moka, Anen's uncle. My brother, the chief, is leading the rest of our people back to our home in the Land of Tall Pines. He wants me to tell you how indebted he is to you for rescuing Anen, his loved daughter."

Winno raised his hand for attention. "At sundown, we hold our feast. We will celebrate with food and games. A mother has found her daughter, and clans have shared knowledge. It is only right to enjoy a celebration."

At once, everyone headed in different directions. Maida went with Anen and her mother.

"We will set up the feast in the meeting place," said Winno to Kael. "The two of you can join the other boys there."

Kael grinned at Gonter. They had to show the boys of this clan a thing or two.

The boys gathered in an open clearing

alongside the meeting place. Kael sized them up. They were big.

“What games do you play?” Gonter asked.

“Do you know Push Over?” replied a tall boy named Jonar. His dark eyes flashed with mischief. The other boys grinned.

Gonter shook his head. “I do not know it, but I will try it.”

The two boys lined up left side to left side, one foot touching, the other foot flat on the ground. They clasped their right hands.

“You can push or pull with your hand to get the other off balance, but you cannot move your feet. Now begin,” cried one of the boys from the Clan of Fierce Faces.

Whomp! Gonter lay on his back on the ground.

“It is easy,” said Jonar, standing over Gonter. He turned and gave Kael a wide smile.

“He is the best at this game,” said one of the boys, clapping Jonar on the back.

Gonter scrambled to his feet. “Let me try that again.”

Jonar pointed at Kael. “Him, first.”

Kael took a deep breath. He had watched Gonter be thrown down and was still trying to figure out how to win. Jonar's height and strength gave him an advantage.

Jonar and Kael lined up, side to side, left feet touching, right hands gripped.

"Begin!" came the cry.

Jonar pushed. Kael pushed back. Suddenly, Jonar pulled away. Within moments, Kael was flat on his back on the ground, staring up at the sky. He heard the laughter of the boys around him and rose to his feet, determined to win.

"Kael, come here," Gonter called.

Kael limped over to him.

"I saw Jonar did," whispered Gonter. "Here is what we need to do..."

"You," said Jonar, pointing to Gonter, interrupting their strategy talk. "You want to try again?"

Gonter nodded and lined up with Jonar.

Jonar pushed.

Gonter pulled back.

Jonar teetered back and forth and pushed against Gonter, then suddenly pulled back.

Gonter was ready. He ducked and pushed against Jonar, using the muscles in his legs to keep his balance.

The tall boy struggled to right himself.

Gonter's legs quivered with the strain of Jonar's weight. He hung on until Jonar tumbled to the ground.

"Ah-h-h," came the cry from the group of boys. "Such strong legs."

Jonar jumped to his feet. A scowl marred his face. "Hey, that was not right. You are supposed to push or pull, not duck down."

"No," said one of the boys, stepping forward. "You know the rules, Jonar. As long as you keep your feet in place, any movement is fair."

"My turn," said Kael. His backside still hurt from where he had been thrown to the ground.

Jonar waved Kael away.

Soon, the boys were involved in a game of Grab the Growler.

Laughter rang out as the feast began to take shape. Delicious aromas of cooking food filled the air. Kael's stomach growled.

"Come. It is time," Winno called to them. Kael raced with the other boys to where Winno stood at the entrance to the shelter.

Winno held up his hand. "Our guests of honor will be seated first."

Anen, her mother Rutti, and her uncle, Moka, were led inside to seats on a log beside Maida.

Kael and Gonter took seats next to them. Winno and the hunters of the clan were seated next. Then Tesi, honored as the wise woman of the clan, took a seat beside Winno. The rest were seated outside the building, where logs had been lined up for the feast.

The women served steaming food in large wooden bowls, carved and painted with different creatures. A young girl handed Kael a bowl of food and gave him a wooden spoon, carved to match the bowl.

"A gift for you," she said quietly and moved on to Gonter.

Kael studied the spoon. The face of Biva was carved on its handle.

He studied Gonter's spoon. His carving was

of a Night Flier.

Winno held up a spoon of his own. “At our feasts, we give gifts to our guests. It is a way for them to remember us.”

“And the story pole is another,” said Doran, the small man who was the carver of the clan.

Kael grinned, remembering how frightened he had been to see the carved Growler. “We thought the Growler on your story pole was real.”

Doran nodded his head in appreciation.

“More food for our guests,” said Winno, beckoning to the women to fill the bowls once more.

Kael ate until his stomach was ready to burst.

Winno leaned back among his furs. A smile played around his lips. “Perhaps Tesi has something to tell our young travelers. Something about Neptu, the King of the Sea.”

“Yes!” came cries from the children. Even the boys Kael’s age leaned forward in anticipation.

Tesi rose and turned in a circle, addressing the crowd. “It is a story for all of us. Especially you. And you. And you,” she said, pointing to a number of wide-eyed children in the audience.

Kael stirred in his seat, wondering what words of wisdom Tesi would offer.

"Beyond where we live," Tesi began, "is something called the Big Water. It is called that because no matter how far one studies it or even travels on it, there is no end in sight. It is truly huge. The Big Water is full of many creatures, none as famous as Neptu. He is the ruler of it all. He is usually a peaceful ruler, allowing the water to come and go from the land as it usually does. Sometimes Neptu becomes angry. Then, the wind howls with his displeasure, and the water washes over the land with a fury to match his. It is said that such a thing sweeps people away. So, when they are by the Big Water, all children need to be as good as they can be, so as not to anger him. If not, Neptu may rise up out of the water and carry them away."

"Aw, that is another one of your scary stories," grumbled Jonar.

Tesi shrugged her shoulders. "I tell what I hear. Only those who go to the Big Water will know for sure." She turned and studied Kael.

A shadow settled on him. Tesi's smile was not reassuring. He exchanged worried glances with Maida and Gonter. What awaited them at the Big Water? Maida's clan was there. Was Neptu waiting for them, too?

CHAPTER SEVEN

Kael stood with Maida and Gonter outside the log house, his furs folded, his carrying sacs full.

Winno joined them. "Ah, my young travelers, I see you are eager to be on your way. I understand. I was young once, and I was curious about the world."

Tesi came over to them. "It is fortunate that you came our way. Your visit will be forever etched into our story pole. We will always remember you, young travelers, the gray Howler, Anen, and the Night Flier. And I think you will remember us."

Gonter held up a spear. "Winno traded this spear for a sling. Now, I can show my people a new way of making them."

"I have shown Doran the picture Serek made for me," Maida announced. "He is going to carve a mask like it."

Tesi nodded. “That will be a new skill for our clan.”

Tesi turned to Kael. She took hold of his hands and closed her eyes. When she opened them, she wore a faraway expression on her wrinkled face. “You may remember your visit to this area for a different reason—perhaps a battle or difficult challenge to overcome.”

Icy fingers gripped Kael’s heart. His life seemed to be one challenge after another. He clutched his spear so hard that his knuckles turned white.

Anen’s mother, Rutti, came up to them, Anen at her side. "Before you leave, I want you to have something from me, a gift from my clan to you for saving Anen and helping to reunite us.”

She handed Kael, Gonter, and Maida each a round piece of ivory. “Moka made these from the horn of a Slasher. Each piece has a figure carved into it, a special symbol of our gratitude."

Kael glanced at the figure of a Night Flier and smiled. He would never forget Owlit and how the bird had saved them from the Gouger.

A wolf was etched into Gonter's piece of

horn. Maida's gift carried the picture of a woodland flower.

Her cheeks wet with tears, Anen gave each of them a hug and left with her mother.

Kael lifted his furs and travel sacs. Maida waved goodbye, and Gonter led Brota out of the village.

As they walked, Tesi's warning rang in Kael's mind. People thought he was brave, but he was terrified when he fought the Gouger by his village, and then later, facing a Gouger with his friends. There would be no Owlit to help them in another fight. Free at last, the Night Flier had flown away before the feast and had not returned.

Darkness stopped them. Rain began to fall. They hurried to gather pine branches for their sleeping places and wove others to form a protective covering above.

Kael and Gonter tied the woven branches between two tree trunks. Maida spread dry branches on the ground beneath, and the three of them and Brota huddled inside. Without a fire, their meal consisted of dried strips of meat and black berries.

To keep their minds off the dangerous animals that might be roaming, they talked about their families. Maida told them about the enjoyment her people had living beside the huge expanse of water. As she talked about the water games she played, the frightening images of Neptu faded from Kael's mind. He could not wait to see the Big Water. Winno had told them it was within reach.

Kael awoke and stretched. The rain had stopped. The sun broke through the overcast sky, highlighting the drops of rain that still clung to the leaves of the trees.

Gonter and Maida were as anxious as Kael to reach the Big Water. They ate an easy meal and packed up.

They had traveled for some distance when they decided to rest beside a creek. Fish leaped playfully in and out of the clear water. Their silvery, tempting skin shone in the sun.

Gonter's eyes lit. He rubbed his stomach.

"Fresh fish."

Kael searched for more firewood while Gonter went about setting up a fire.

Catching fish was one of Maida's skills. She waded into the water and stood still, waiting for a fish to swim close by. In one smooth movement, she trapped a fish with a piece of animal skin, flung it onto the bank of the stream, and stood ready to catch another.

Soon, three good-sized fish lay on the ground.

While Gonter and Maida gutted and cleaned them, Kael walked along the creek's edge, searching for a large flat stone. They had learned that if they set such a stone in hot coals and placed fish on top of it with a sprinkling of water, it would turn out to be nice and moist.

Walking head down, he searched for the perfect rock. He had just rounded a bend in the stream when he found a large, flat stone big enough to hold three fish, thin enough to carry. It lay in the shallow, clear water ahead of him. He bent over to lift it out and stiffened at the sound of a roar nearby. One he had hoped never to hear again.

The blood left his face so fast he felt woozy.

He whipped around.

The largest brown Growler Kael had ever seen stood on hind legs on the bank of the stream, growling ferociously.

Kael's fingers crept up to touch his father's bear claw necklace. His heart pounded with such fear that his body became weak.

"Kael? Where are you?"

The sound of Gonter's voice hung in the air, freezing both the Growler's movement and his own. Kael could not answer. Not with his mouth dry with fright.

Gonter appeared in the distance. Fear shot through Kael. Words pushed through his throat in a panic. "Do not come any closer. It is a Growler!"

The Growler swiveled its attention from Gonter to Kael and back again.

Foolishly, Kael had left his spear and sling back by the fire. He scooped up stones from the creek bed. "Run, Gonter! I will distract him." He took aim at the Growler. "Get out of here! Go,

Growler! You do not need to hurt us."

A spot of brown, half hidden in the tall grass at the water's edge, caught Kael's attention. A baby Growler peered up out of the grass at him. He held onto the stone he was about to throw. The female Growler was protecting her baby, like the Growler that had killed his father.

Kael backed up, easing away slowly. "I see your baby," he crooned. "I will not hurt it if you let me leave. See? I am moving away."

At the last moment, Kael could not help himself. He turned and ran as fast as he could, his breath coming in and out in loud gasps. He caught up with Gonter and did not stop running until he reached their campsite some distance away.

Trembling, Kael collapsed on the ground beside the fire. Images of his father facing a Growler played in his mind.

"What happened? What is wrong?" said Maida.

Sprawled on the ground beside Kael, Gonter said, "It was the biggest Growler I have ever seen."

"She was protecting her baby," Kael said, trying to calm his racing heart. His legs shook so badly he could not hold them still.

Gonter clapped him on the back. "You saved my life, Kael. I do not know how you did it. You talked that Growler into letting us go. It was a brave thing to do."

Brave? Kael sat up in surprise. He had run like one of the horned animals of the woods. He touched his necklace. Others may think he was brave, but he knew he would never be as brave as his father.

Instead of cooking the fish on a stone, they wrapped strips of fish around sticks and cooked them over the fire. The pink-fleshed fish was accompanied by small blackberries Maida had found among the bushes clustered along the banks of the creek.

As he packed up to leave, Kael could not help glancing around for signs of other Growlers. He was relieved when they filled their water sacs and left.

Their hiking became easier as the forest thinned, and the hills rolled more gently.

Anxious to see her family, Maida urged them on.

They settled for the night in a grove of trees.

"We are getting close." Maida's voice filled with happiness as she helped Kael prepare a soup of meat and herbs.

He nodded, understanding her excitement. He thought of his mother and sister, wondering where they were, if they were all right, and when he would see them again. He, as he always did at moments like this, vowed to find them.

Breezes blew steadily as they walked in the early light. Nose high, Brota bounded ahead of them.

Gonter stopped and sniffed the air. "Something smells different."

Maida lifted her face and inhaled, then clapped her hands. "It is the Big Water! I would know that smell anywhere."

Kael breathed in the salty tang.

"Listen!" said Gonter.

A muffled roar filled the air, a roar that grew loud then softened in a rhythmic pattern.

Maida grinned. "Race you to the water."

The three of them hoisted their packs and began to run through scrub brushes and trees. Brota sprinted ahead.

Kael came to an abrupt halt. White ground lay ahead of him. Beyond it, gray-blue water rose and fell in wave after wave.

"What is it?" Kael stooped to grab a handful of the white substance, expecting to find it cold and wet like the snow in the Land of Fire and Ice. It was warm and soft. He sifted the light-colored material through his fingers.

Gonter kicked off his leather foot coverings and wiggled his toes in a strange substance.

"It is sand," giggled Maida, taking off her foot coverings.

Kael removed the leather from his feet in one swift motion and burrowed his feet into its softness.

Laughing, the three of them leapt about and twirled in a circle until they collapsed in a heap.

Maida lay back on the sand, smiling. "I knew you would like it."

Gonter sat up. "Is the Big Water warm, too?"

“See for yourself.” Her dark eyes sparkled with mischief.

Side by side, they walked to the edge of the water. As far as Kael could see, blue waves rolled in to touch the sandy shore and retreat, as if the waves were playing a game of tag.

He dipped his toe into the water and leapt back as water rolled toward him. Droplets of water covered his legs and sprayed the leather he wore around his waist. He gasped at its coldness.

A wave knocked Gonter over. Water dripped from his blond locks and ran down his cheeks as he slowly regained his balance. His breath came out in little puffs of surprise that made Kael laugh.

Maida stood on the beach at the water’s edge. Water splashed over her toes in little waves. She glanced over at the boys and smiled. “You will get used to it. The waves come and go, but they will not hurt you. Boys and girls in our clan ride them on pieces of wood.”

The water curled in front of Kael and rolled toward him. He stepped back, not ready to ride any waves.

“We need to keep going,” Maida said. “My clan must be nearby. I remember those huge rocks over there.”

They picked up their things and began walking barefoot in the sand. They had not gone far when Gonter stopped.

“What is that?”

“It is one of our dugouts!” Maida cried. She dropped her sacs and waved frantically at the large wooden boat.

When it began to head their way, Maida jumped up and down on the sand and clapped her hands. “They see me. Here they come!”

As the boat drew nearer, Kael observed several men kneeling inside it, paddling. One man stood at the back and directed the others.

The boat rode the waves ashore, gliding onto the sand and stopping halfway out of the water.

Maida splashed through the water, shouting, “Dada, I am here!”

The man who had been standing in the back of the boat leaped over the side of it and waded ashore. Maida threw herself into her father's arms. Even from a distance, Kael could see the joy in her father's face as he hugged Maida. His eyes watered at the memory of his father's arms around him.

A young boy jumped out of the front of the boat and began tugging on it each time a wave rolled ashore. Soon, the boat settled on the edge of the sand. The rest of the people stayed in the boat, staring at them.

Kael studied the boat. It was carved out of a huge tree trunk. The sides appeared to be thin but sturdy. The room inside the boat was plentiful. Kael wondered how long it took to hollow out a tree like that. His clan had heard of large dugout boats like this. They had never made one because the river beside them was too shallow to handle it.

The boy who had helped move the boat closer to shore swaggered over to Kael and Gonter. "Who are you? And why are you traveling with Maida?" he asked.

Gonter frowned. "We are traveling together as part of a plan."

"So, who are you?" the boy repeated.

Kael stepped forward. "I am Kael, and this is

my friend Gonter. Who exactly are you?"

The boy lifted his chin. "I am Damo, the chief's son. Do not forget it!"

At the boy's bold words, Kael felt his cheeks grow hot. He held his tongue and glanced at Gonter, whose frown had deepened into lines of annoyance.

"Dada, here are my friends, Kael and Gonter," cried Maida.

She and her father approached them.

Maida's father held up his right hand in greeting. 'I am Hetar. Thank you for helping Maida travel to us. She told me you are the young ones Grandfather dreamed about. It is good to meet you. Come. We will take you with us." He pointed to Brota. "Is it safe to be with him?"

Gonter patted Brota on the head. "He will not hurt anyone unless they try to hurt him."

Hetar nodded. "Then he can come in the boat with us."

Gonter shook his head. "I am not sure he will do that. He did not like the Walking River."

"We will let him try," said Hetar. "Come. My people will take you to our home."

Home. Kael gathered up his things. He wondered what kind of home he would find at the edge of the Big Water. He followed the others into the shallow water and loaded his things into the boat.

At Hetar's instruction, Kael crawled over the side of the dugout and settled on its wooden bottom. Gonter climbed in beside him.

"Here, Brota. Come!" Gonter waved the wolf forward. Brota whined but would not come all the way into the water. He bit the waves at his feet and shook his head when droplets splashed on his muzzle.

"We will stay close to land so your pet can follow us on shore," said Hetar, helping Maida aboard.

As they prepared to leave, anticipation filled Kael. He huddled beside Gonter and Maida. "Pull away," Hetar commanded.

The eight men began to paddle backwards in unison.

Kael's stomach fluttered as the boat slowly edged away from the shore. It was a new adventure–riding on top of the Big Water in a boat bigger than anything he had ever seen.

A wave rocked the boat, making it tilt.

Panic shot through Kael. He grabbed onto the side of the boat.

Damo glanced back at him and shot him a scornful glance.

Kael managed to make a shaky smile, determined that Damo would not see the fear that continued to fill him. He glanced at Gonter and could tell by the furrows on his brow that he was worried about tipping over, too.

Maida spoke quietly to them. "It takes a while to get used to being on the water. The boat is built to be safe. That is why it has such a wide bottom."

Kael relaxed and began to enjoy the rocking motion of the boat. The men hummed as they swung their paddles in and out of the water to the rhythm of the song Maida's father sang. Kael's heart lifted. It was a little bit like flying.

The boat rounded the rocks Maida had seen in the distance. Brota stood at the end of the rocky point of land and howled. Then he ran back along the shore, following their progress as they pulled into a sandy cove.

The waves helped push the boat ashore. Damo jumped out of the boat and helped guide it even closer, wave by wave.

On shore, members of Maida's clan gathered and scanned the passengers in the boat. One woman, carrying a baby, stepped forward.

"Maida, my daughter. You have come at last!"

Maida climbed out of the boat and into her mother's arms. Her mother drew her close and kissed her again and again.

Gonter patted Brota and said quietly to Kael, "This is an interesting place."

Kael nodded. New adventures awaited them.

CHAPTER EIGHT

Maida's mother approached them. "I am Noona. I welcome you to our clan," she said formally. "While you are here, you will be like my own. Everything I have, I offer you. You have given me the greatest gift of all—the safe return of my daughter."

She patted Gonter's cheek and then Kael's. "Thank you, my son," she murmured to each of them and walked away.

Maida trotted over to them, carrying her baby sister. "This is Kali. She is not yet one whole season. My mother sent my brother, Cuja to Grandfather's home to ask me to come and help take care of her."

Kali stared at the boys with round, dark eyes. A smile burst across her face when Brota came closer and sniffed her curiously. She clapped her hands with glee.

Brota wagged his tail and let out an ear-splitting yip.

Kali's cooing sounds turned into a loud wail.

Maida's mother took Kali from Maida. "Why not show the boys our warm home?"

Kael and Gonter followed Maida to a hut. The structure was made of bent sticks tied together and covered with animal skins. Several other huts lined the edge of the woods overlooking the beach.

Inside, sleeping platforms were set above the ground, allowing storage spaces underneath them to be used.

"Each family has their own house," Maida said.

"My clan lives that way, too," said Kael, feeling at home in the space she assigned to him.

Damo swaggered inside. "You, both of you boys, come. It is time for you to meet the others."

Kael glanced at Maida uncertainly.

Damo tapped his foot. "*Now.*"

"Go," Maida said. "He will not stop until you do what he wants. He always gets his way."

Kael bit back a reply. He had never met

anyone as annoying as Damo.

A group of boys had gathered outside the hut.

"Here they are," announced Damo. "These are the visitors Maida brought with her."

A boy gave his name as Gropa. "You have been traveling with Maida? How is it, being one of the girls?"

The boys laughed.

Kael's cheeks burned. "Maida is a skilled hunter and a worthy companion."

"She even saved our lives in the Land of Fire and Ice," Gonter said, frowning fiercely. "We might have been killed without her help."

Kael noticed the boys' looks of surprise and was satisfied.

"Maida's grandfather made certain she was taught to hunt and fish, but she will never really be one of us," said Damo. He turned to the others, seeking their agreement.

A few of the boys studied the ground and shuffled their feet. The others nodded. It pleased Kael that Maida had a few friends among the group.

"So, let us see how good you are," said Damo.

"Do you know the game 'Push Over'?"

At the gleam in Gonter's eyes, Kael smiled to himself. They might have a chance to put Damo in his place.

"Sure. Want to play?" asked Gonter.

Damo nodded. "I am the best at it."

Gonter and Damo lined up, side by side, one foot touching, like Gonter and Kael had learned from the boys in the Clan of Fierce Faces.

"He had better let Damo win," Gropa whispered to Kael.

Kael shook his head. "That would not be fair."

Gripping hands, Gonter and Damo see-sawed back and forth and shifted weight from one foot to the other, trying to keep their balance and knock the other one over. In moments, Damo lay on the ground.

"Guess I win this time," said Gonter proudly. He offered a hand to Damo.

Damo slapped Gonter's hand away and jumped to his feet, his face red with fury. "You moved your feet or did something else to cheat. I *never* lose."

Gonter scowled. “I play fair. You lost this once, Damo.”

“No.” Damo turned to his fellow clan members. “He cheated.”

“No, Damo,” said Gropa. “He beat you fairly.”

Damo stamped his foot. “You lie, Gropa.”

Kael spoke in the quiet that followed Damo’s accusation. “The game was played like we were taught. Do you want to give *me* a try?”

Damo shook his head. “I do not trust you. Come, boys. We will leave our visitors to the girls. That is where they belong.”

Several of the boys followed Damo.

Gropa stayed behind. “A word of advice,” he told Kael and Gonter. “No one wants to speak up to Damo. His father, Chief Vukon, is a fair man, but he believes everything Damo tells him. He does not understand what Damo is like with others. In every other way, Vukon is an excellent leader of our people.” Gropa held up a finger in warning. “You never heard such words from me."

Kael nodded, not at all certain he could play by Damo’s rules. Grumbling softly to each other, he and Gonter returned to Maida's house,

Maida's mother wrapped several pieces of fish in seaweed and laid them on a flat stone in the coals of the fire. Maida's father appeared and took a seat on a log near the fire. He motioned the boys closer.

"Tell us about yourselves."

Kael and Gonter filled him in on how they had come to travel together.

"I am sorry about your family, Kael," Hetar said.

"We met Maida in the Land of Fire and Ice," said Gonter. "She saved our lives from three evil hunters who would kill us to prevent us from going to the Beast with the Golden Horn."

"She is a skilled hunter and a worthy companion. The three of us have become close friends, depending on one another," Kael said. "We are part of Grandfather's dreams."

"I am proud of my daughter," said Maida's father, placing a hand on her shoulder. "And I am glad that as you three have traveled, you were eager to learn things from others," Hetar said. "My father, Maida's grandfather, always told me it was necessary to share information if our people were to survive in a changing world. He has had such thoughts for many, many seasons."

"He is very wise," said Kael. "He knew about us even before Gonter and I came to the Land of Fire and Ice."

"Yes. He is the wisest man in our clan. That is why we allowed Maida stay behind with him," said Maida's father. "It was as he had dreamed."

"Can you tell us about your boats?" Gonter asked. "My people live in the mountains and have never seen large boats like yours."

Hetar nodded. A smile of satisfaction appeared on his face. "I will show you how we make them. It is something you should learn while you are staying with us at the Big Water."

Kael grinned. Once he got used to its rocking motion, he would like riding in the large dugout boat.

At sunrise, Maida's father said, "I will take you into the woods so you can see how the boats are made. We are making a small one for the young boys of our clan so they can learn how to handle a dugout. The men can use their help to catch a Spouter."

"What's a Spouter?" Gonter asked.

"It is a huge creature that lives in the Big Water. We call them Spouters because they blow air and water through an opening at the top of their heads. The oil from them is used for many things, such as treating animal skin and lighting fires. They are not easy to catch. It takes many men and a lot of cooperation to bring in one Spouter."

Kael studied the movement of the Big Water and wondered what others lived there. His thoughts turned to Neptu. He wondered if there was such a living thing. A shiver crossed his shoulders.

"Come. We will go now." Maida's father led them into the trees behind the huts.

In the middle of a clearing lay a large log, partially hollowed out.

"Sometimes we roll a log to the sandy beach and do our work there. We are leaving this one here to make sure it is light enough for the boys to carry," Hetar explained. "First, we hollow out spots along the log and set a fire in each one. The burn is controlled by pouring water on the blaze. After we let it dry, we begin our carving."

Hetar took them over to where a number of men were working. He pointed out a man holding an unusually large stone hatchet.

“Comer is our master carver. He designs our boats. This one is smaller and lighter than the others, but Comer says it will work. He has created new carving tools for this project, using thinner and sharper stones than the ones we typically use.

“I also use shells from the Big Water to carve out the boat. The ones that are big and have curling edges can be used to dig out ashes from the burn. You will see,” said Comer.

“See, Hetar!” A young boy approached them. “See what I have made.”

Maida’s father knelt and accepted a piece of wood from the thin boy.

“It is exactly like a Spouter, Parni.” Hetar turned to the boys. “This is Parni, Damo’s younger brother.”

Kael hid his surprise. In physical appearance

and behavior, this boy bore little resemblance to his bullying older brother.

Parni's lower lip stuck out in a pout as he handed the carving to Kael. "Damo thinks I am a baby because I like to carve things. I am no baby. I do not like the way he plays."

Kael could well imagine the taunting Damo would give his younger brother. Damo, with his whining, spoiled ways, would never understand a gentle person like Parni. He certainly would not appreciate Parni's beautiful work.

Kael traced the smooth curve of the Spouter's wooden body with his fingers. "Have you seen the story poles of the People of Fierce Faces?"

Parni nodded. "From a distance. They are huge."

"Why not make a miniature one, so your clan can tell a story, too," said Gonter.

Parni's eyes widened. "If I make it small enough, it can be carried back and forth from here to the Land of Fire and Ice." He clicked his fingers. "I have an even better idea. I will show you later. For now, it is my secret."

He hurried away.

Hetar gave Gonter a nod of approval. “An exchange of ideas is wise.”

Kael and Gonter spent a long time watching Comer and other men of the clan work on the boat. Boatmaking was a long process, but an important one.

Maida appeared a while later. “Let’s go down to the Big Water. I will show you how to ride the waves.”

Kael and Gonter eagerly followed Maida to her house. She gave each of them a wide, flat piece of log. “You will need these,” she said, and led them down to the water’s edge.

Damo and a group of boys were already in the water. Mindful of the boys watching him, Kael held back a shout as his feet hit the cold waves.

“Hurry!” said Maida. She ran into the water and stood waist-deep in it. “A big wave is coming.”

A curl of water crested behind her. As the tip of the curl reached her, she flung herself on top of the piece of wood she held and let the wave carry her to shore.

Kael followed her back into the water. As a wave rushed toward him, he flung himself on the board. Instead of gliding toward the shore, the power of the wave shoved him underwater. He was gasping for air when his face broke through the water's surface. He spit out the bad-tasting water that he had caught in his mouth.

Damo's mocking voice greeted him. "What a baby."

Kael gritted his teeth, stood, and faced another wave. Damo's taunt reminded him of Borlan, the bully back home, whose curse Kael was forced to carry with him. Determined to do better, Kael waited until the right moment, then turned and rode the crest of the wave toward shore.

Gonter rode on a board alongside Kael.

Kael stood in the shallow water, smiling happily.

Damo strode toward them, followed by a group of his loyal followers. He smirked. "What are you two doing playing with a girl?"

Damo's dutiful followers laughed.

“Ignore him,” Gonter whispered to Kael.

Damo waved his friends forward. The group of boys surrounded Kael and Gonter in the water. One of them, a tall boy, dunked Kael beneath the water, holding his head down.

Kael fought him off and punched him in the belly.

Soon, all of the boys were fighting.

“Stop!” shouted Maida, striding over to them. “Do not hurt my friends.”

Damo pointed a finger at her. “Go play with the other girls instead of trying to be like us boys.”

“She is a better person than you,” said Kael.

“If I leave, will you stop being cruel to my friends?” said Maida.

Damo laughed and nodded towards Kael and Gonter. “You mean these babies?”

“They are not babies, Damo. They are far better boys than you will ever be.” Maida’s dark eyes flashed with anger.

“Nobody is better than me,” said Damo. “Even my father thinks so.”

“Your father does not see how you really

are," said Maida. "*You* are a baby."

Damo's expression turned ugly. "I am no baby. Do not forget it! You should never have been taught to hunt like us boys. It has made you... you...wrong! That is what."

Maida gave one last glance at Kael and Gonter and left, hoping the boys would stop fighting.

"Good job, Damo," said one of the boys.

Kael watched Maida leave and wondered why so many of the boys in the clan followed Damo's rule. Were they afraid of him, or did they find it easier to follow someone else than to fight for their own thoughts? Either way, the situation was bad.

Kael waded out of the water, and Gonter followed. Their time with the water boards had been ruined.

As they were walking away, Damo jumped on Kael's back. Furious, Kael swung around and threw Damo to the ground.

"Get them!" cried Damo, rising to his feet. The other boys simply stared with awe at Kael.

Gonter faced Damo. "It is cowardly to attack

from behind."

Kael and Gonter once more walked away from the group of boys. The skin on Kael's back felt as if a snake was crawling on it. He vowed to keep walking without showing any fear.

CHAPTER NINE

As Kael and Gonter returned to Maida's home, Brota pranced at their sides.

"How are you?" asked Maida.

"We got the best of Damo," Kael told her.

Maida shook her head. "It is not a good thing to be better than Damo. He will never forgive you."

"What can he do to us?" challenged Gonter. "We will be here for only a short time."

Maida shrugged.

Kael took her words to heart. He did not like Damo—or trust him.

Kael and Gonter stood in the woods with the boys of the clan, watching Comer and the other men work on the dugout. After several sunrises, the small boat for hunting and fishing excursions grew closer to being ready.

Comer explained how important it was to

carve the log in such a way that the wooden sides and bottom of the boat were thin and therefore lighter than normal, but still broad enough and thick enough to be stable. Both ends of the boat were pointed, making it easier for it to travel through the water.

Damo had been chosen to take the spot at the back of the boat, singing and calling out orders, as Hetar did for the men.

"It will take cooperation among the twelve boys inside to move it through the water and keep it steady," Comer said. He gave Damo a silent warning.

"I am the best leader in the clan," said Damo. "Everyone knows enough to follow me."

Kael and Gonter exchanged glances. Damo could not stop bragging.

At last, the boat was ready. The men instructed the boys of the clan to carry it from the woods to the edge of the water.

Excited, the boys gathered around it.

"I know you want to get into the boat right now," Chief Vukon said. “You must wait. It cannot be used until we have a proper ceremony.

At sundown, we will celebrate the completion of the boat."

Later, as the sun prepared to dip below the horizon, the entire clan gathered around a huge bonfire on the beach. The women organized a community meal. Families stood or sat, sampling the grilled fish, the berry and nut mixtures, and the fern soup. Young children ran in circles or splashed in the water near the shore.

Kael and Gonter stood among the older boys surrounding the boat, as anxious as they were for the ceremony to begin. Chief Vukon had given permission to both of them to join the maiden voyage.

Vukon rose to address the clan. “This is a special occasion. It is the first time we have made a boat especially for our young hunters. This watercraft will be used to learn about the sea and how to hunt successfully on the water. We are a small group. We need our young hunters to become skilled so we can all be well fed.”

The chief laid a hand on the front of the boat. “All of us in this clan give our blessing to this boat, asking for protection for the young men who will use it. I say young men, for those among them who are selected to join the last hunt before we return to the Land of Fire and Ice will be young men, not boys, in our eyes."

Damo grinned and nudged several boys around him. "I will be the leader on that hunt. Wait and see."

Kael rolled his eyes at Gonter.

Chief Vukon cleared his throat. "We have another blessing to bestow on this boat. Parni, step forward."

All eyes turned to the young boy, who handed three wooden paddles to Vukon. The chief held them up for all to see.

The blades were wide and smooth. The shafts were long and narrow. At the tip of each shaft was a design carved into the handle, created so that a hand could fit over it nicely.

"While Comer and his group were busy working on the boat, Parni and his teacher, Sonda, have been creating the necessary paddles for the hunters," said Chief Vukon.

"Baby stuff," whispered Damo, loud enough

for Kael and others to hear.

Chief Vukon scowled at Damo and continued. “Three of them have been created with special carvings. Kael, Gonter, and Damo, come forward.”

Parni handed a paddle to Gonter, one to Kael, and one to Damo.

“We have two special visitors from other clans," said Chief Vukon. "It is good that we share ideas. Gonter suggested that Parni carve stories into things, like the Clan of Fierce Faces do with their story poles.”

Chief Vukon took the paddle from Kael and held it up. “This has a Spouter carved on it. Parni said Kael would know why he was given this particular one.”

Kael smiled. He knew it was because he had not teased Parni about the wooden Spouter the young boy had carved.

Gonter’s paddle had a Howler remarkably like Brota carved into its handle.

Damo held up his paddle. “Mine's the best. It has a Growler on it.”

A Growler? Kael’s stomach clenched.

Though he had escaped the mother protecting her baby, the image of the Growler who had killed his father hovered in his mind.

Someone in the group beat on a hollow log with a stick. The sound trembled in the air, like an exciting promise. The waves of the water hitting the sand made another rhythmic sound.

Hetar's voice sang out.

> "*Blessed is the deep blue sea*
> *We sing our joy on bended knee*
> *Dip, pull, and glide, dip, pull, and glide*
> *Through rolling waves, we go with pride.*"

Hetar moved his feet to the music, up and down.

Other men followed.

Soon, a whole circle of men danced around the fire to the musical beat of the sticks on the hollow wood.

The women and children began to clap to the rhythm. Other voices sang the sea chant over and over again.

The Chief gathered seawater in a gourd and dribbled it down the length of the boat, adding a blessing of the sea.

When the singing stopped, he held up his hands. "At sunrise, the boys will take the boat on the water."

A cheer rose up from the clan, and then people moved away to their houses for the dark time.

Later, in the darkness of Maida's home, Kael tossed and turned on his furs, too excited to sleep. He and Gonter would go in the boat with the other boys. It was a new experience, and they had to do well.

"I wish I could go in the boat with you," Maida whispered from across the room.

"We will tell you all about it," said Kael. "Then, you might be able to go another time."

"As long as Damo is the leader of the boat, he will not allow it. Grandfather is not here to defend me."

Kael heard the sadness in Maida's voice. "After we learn how to handle the boat, it is possible Chief Vukon will let us take you out in it."

"I am not certain of that," she answered despondently, and rolled over.

Kael lay back on his furs. Maida had been an able traveling companion. She had carried her share of the load, cooked her share of the meals, and had hunted well. She had even saved his life. He could easily imagine how it must hurt to suddenly be forbidden to do those things. He was glad he was going in the boat. It was unfortunate that Damo was their leader.

At sunup, the boys gathered around the dugout on the beach with Hetar. Curious members of the clan stayed to one side to observe.

"Damo," said Hetar, "stand here by me." He signaled the others. "We need six boys on one side of the boat, five on the other. Grab hold of it. There are handholds carved into the side of the boat to make it easier for you. When I say 'go', lift up the boat and move forward to the edge of the water."

Hetar turned to Damo. "When the boat is resting at the water's edge, climb aboard. Sing out the song, like I taught you. It will set the rhythm for the others. They will need it to backpaddle the boat and get it turned around."

"I know how," grumbled Damo, glancing at the group watching them. "You do not have to tell me."

Hetar patted him on the back. "Do as I say." He turned to the boys holding onto the dugout. "Go!"

All together, they lifted the boat. Grunting and groaning, they managed to half-drag, half-carry it to the water's edge.

Hetar motioned to Damo. "Hop in, so you can direct the others."

Damo crawled into the boat and moved to the back, where a seat had been carved for him.

Hetar addressed the other boys. "Watch the waves and follow their pattern, pushing the boat into the water as a wave rolls back. As soon as you are waist-deep in the water, climb into the boat. Those standing at the bow will be the last ones in."

Kael and Gonter, at the front end of the boat, hopped in as Damo shouted for the crew to paddle backwards as hard as they could.

There was confusion as each boy swung his paddle at a different time.

"Stop shouting and start singing," Hetar called out to Damo. "Get a rhythm going."

The boat turned sideways and rolled from side to side with the movement of the waves.

Gropa suddenly sang out the boating chant. "Dip, pull, glide. Dip, pull, glide."

The boat began to face the waves, the way it was supposed to.

Damo rose from his seat and whacked Gropa on the back with his paddle.

The singing stopped, the boat turned sideways and flipped over.

"Do not let the boat go," shouted Hetar as he and the other men waded into the water to help.

Damo stormed out of the water and marched past the group gathered on the shore.

"Stop!" shouted Hetar. "Damo, come back."

Damo turned around. "It was not my fault the boat tipped over. It was Gropa's fault."

Damo started to walk away, but his father stopped him. "Return to the others," he said in a quiet, stern voice heard by all.

This time, Damo could not lie about what happened. Though he was forced to join the others, he refused to help turn the boat over and bring it to shore.

After much struggling, the boat was brought back to the water's edge, ready to go.

"All right," said Hetar to Damo. "We are going to try this again. This time, instead of yelling, sing out the rhythm right away."

"Gropa ruined it," said Damo. "I am the leader of the boat. Not him."

"I am the leader of all the boatmen," said Hetar, "and you will do as you are told. No shouting of orders. The chant is how we get people to work together. If you do as I ask, no one else will need to step in and help. Now, let us see you do it. And remember, this is only a practice run, so stay close to shore."

The boys waited until the waves had crashed onto the shore. Then, they hurried to push the boat out with the waves and climb in.

Damo sang out the rhythm.

Working together, the boys pulled the boat

away from the shore and slowly turned it. Then, they headed out into open water.

Kael smiled as he dipped his paddle in the water and pulled hard, doing his share to move the boat forward. Land became a shadow in the distance. In their excitement, the boys had paddled out much farther than they should.

Kael glanced over the side of the boat into the deep blue water, wondering what sort of creatures lived there. Distracted, Kael's paddle hit the one behind him. He worked hard to regain the rhythm.

Damo stopped singing and shouted, "Hey, you! Kael! Stop it! You are not listening to me. You should not be in the boat. You are not one of us."

Kael's face turned hot. He bit back a retort. Damo was itching for a fight. He had been in a bad mood ever since his father and Hetar had forced him to obey.

Gonter whispered, "Do not say anything, Kael. Ignore him."

Kael turned and stared silently at Damo. Movement behind the boat caught his eye.

“Another boat is heading right for us."

Everyone turned around to see.

"Oh, oh," said Damo. "It is the Clan of Raging Waters. That is their red war symbol on the boat."

"Hetar told us to stay close to the village. We are out too far," Gropa said. "We are in trouble now.”

Damo snarled, "I am the leader, not you, Gropa, or anyone else. You will do what I say." He shook his fist. "That means all of you. Keep going!"

"You better not get us in trouble," grumbled Gropa. He picked up his paddle and waited for Damo to begin the chant.

Damo's voice rang out loud and clear. "Dip, pull, glide."

The boys moved as one, sending the dugout up and over the waves in a hurry to get away. No matter how hard the boys paddled, they could not outrun the boat following them.

It moved closer and closer.

The warriors rowed up beside them and grabbed hold of the boys’ boat.

"What do you think you are doing?" roared a huge man with a red beard that matched the wild curls on his head.

"Stay away from us!" shouted Damo. "I am the son of Chief Vukon!"

"You are a foolish little boy," the man replied. "We are not after you. If we were, you would all be in the water wondering what had happened."

The men in his boat laughed.

"See those clouds?" the red-bearded man said, pointing to the sky. "That is not an ordinary storm coming our way. It is a typhu. Turn around and go back to your settlement. Go, now!"

Kael studied the boiling dark clouds heading their way. They were moving fast—faster than the boys could paddle.

"We told you to turn around earlier," Gropa said to Damo. "Now it is too late. We will never make it back in time."

"Listen to me," said Damo. "Begin paddling. We have to try to beat the storm."

The boys paddled as fast as they could. Dip,

pull, glide. Dip, pull, glide.

Kicked up by the wind, the water around them grew rougher. Waves rose up and over the bow of the boat, splashing Kael and Gonter, and filling the boat with water. To keep from going overboard, Kael and Gonter stopped paddling and clung to the sides of the boat.

"Keep paddling!" Damo screamed at them.

"We cannot!" Kael shouted when another wave splashed over him. The bow of the boat dipped into the water, making it impossible for him to even try to paddle.

The wind howled. Kael thought of the story Tesi had told them about Neptu's anger. Their boat tipped from one side to the other as wave after wave struck them. The other boys huddled in the middle of the boat, fighting to keep the boat upright.

"Watch out!" shrieked Gonter.

A huge wall of water rolled toward them.

Kael braced himself, then his hands were swept away from the side of the boat. Helpless against the weight of the water pushing him, he felt his body lifted up, up, up.

Gonter grabbed hold of his arm. Straining for air, they tumbled down through the water.

They reached the surface of the frothy water together. Kael gasped for breath and frantically pumped his arms and legs to try to stay above the rolling surface.

The boat bobbed in the water ahead of them.

“Come,” he said to Gonter. “We can reach it.”

They started swimming.

Damo saw them and shouted to the others, "Keep paddling."

Horrified, Kael watched the boat travel farther and farther away from him.

"I cannot swim anymore," Gonter said, splashing in the water beside him. "It is too hard, and I am too tired."

"You cannot stop," puffed Kael. His arms felt as if they had big rocks tied to them. "We have to try and make it to shore."

Gonter shook his head. "Kael, it is hopeless. We cannot even see the shore from here."

Kael grabbed Gonter under his arms. "I will hold you above the water. We cannot give up."

Try as he might, Kael grew too tired to help

either Gonter or himself. His limbs grew numb in the cold water, and he became groggy.

Darkness closed in.

CHAPTER TEN

On the shore, Maida and her family gathered with other members of her clan, waiting for the boys' boat to return. The cool, howling wind whipped at them fiercely, taking Maida’s breath away. White froth edged the high waves that rolled toward them and pounded on the shore like an angry fist.

Brota whined at Maida's side. She patted him and said to her father, "Something is wrong. Brota knows it, too."

"I thought Damo understood they were to stay near shore.” Hetar shook his head. “When the storm came up, they were so far out to sea that we could do nothing to help them."

"See?" shouted someone. "A boat! I think it is them."

Huddled together in the rain, the group moved closer to the water's edge, straining to see better.

"It *is* our boat," said Maida's father.

"Thanks to the gods!" said Chief Vukon. "I thought they were lost to us."

Mothers wept and fathers heaved sighs of relief that their children were coming home. Younger children raced in circles with excitement. Brota continued whining at Maida's side.

Her heart pounded with foreboding.

The dugout boat approached the shore. The men fought ferocious waves to bring it in. Some of the boys aboard the boat were too sick from the bouncing waves to help. Fighting the bad weather and the rough water, the men edged the boat close enough to shore for the boys to leap out. Mothers raced to embrace their sons who had survived the terrifying storm. The boys came ashore and stood with their families.

Maida tugged on her father's arm. "Where are Kael and Gonter?"

Maida's father, Hetar, approached Damo. "Where are our visitors?"

Damo shook his head. "A wave washed them out of the boat. We could do nothing to help them."

Hetar narrowed his eyes at Damo. Damo looked away.

Tears ran down Maida's cheeks. "I *knew* something was wrong. I *knew* it."

Hetar put his arm around her. "I am sorry, daughter."

Even as tears flowed, determination filled Maida. "I will not give up on them. Brota and I will keep searching for them."

Kael stirred. Something, a light of some sort, woke him. He moaned and sat up. He patted his legs and wiggled his toes.

He was alive!

Kael rubbed his eyes to get a better idea of his surroundings. Rough stone walls formed a dome around him. Water dribbled down them, spreading sparkling little rainbows formed by the light of flaming torches mounted on the walls.

Gonter, I have to find Gonter. Kael rose from the soft dirt where he lay. His legs were unsteady, but he was able to make his way to a doorway into a connecting room. Gonter lay sprawled on the ground, breathing noisily. Kael hurried over to his side.

"Gonter, wake up."

Gonter rolled over. "Huh? Where are we?"

"In a cave of sorts."

Gonter rubbed his eyes. "There are so many colors. Is it magical, like the home of the Light Master?"

"We need to find out where we are," Kael said.

"The last thing I remember was swimming in the water during the storm." Gonter rubbed his head. "How did we get here?"

Kael shrugged. "I do not know."

The sound of singing filled the air, high, lilting notes that echoed against the stone walls, forming a sweet chorus.

"Listen," whispered Gonter.

"Let's see what it is," said Kael, helping Gonter to his feet.

They staggered into another room. In the center of it, dazzling light lit a huge, steaming pool of water. The water running down the stone walls sent colors dancing from place to place and shimmering on the surface of the water.

Kael blinked and smiled. It *was* magical.

"Who are you?" came a high voice.

Kael glanced around but did not see anyone. He turned to Gonter. “Did you say something?”

"No, she did." Gonter pointed above them.

A miniature girl, not bigger than Kael’s hand, fluttered in the air. Her hair was a sunny yellow, and her eyes were like the little violet flowers that grew in the woods near his home. She wore a gown of greenery... and a frown. "I said, ‘Who are you?’”

Kael stared at the little one. The rapid movement of her transparent wings kept her suspended above them.

"I am Kael, and this is my friend, Gonter. Who are you?"

"I am Fari, the head of Neptu's helpers," she answered with pride.

"Neptu? Is he here?" Kael swallowed hard. They had been warned about him.

"He is away, seeing who else we can rescue," said Fari. "You are from the storm."

"Where are we?" asked Kael.

Fari let out a high, trilling laugh, like a soft aria. "In Neptu's home."

Kael and Gonter sat at the edge of the steamy pool. The room suddenly filled with many creatures like Fari. They flew in circles around the boys' heads, filling the air with their laughter.

"They are so big, for boys," said a little one, hovering in front of Kael. She reached out a tiny finger and touched his nose. Against his skin, it felt like the wings of a butterfly.

"This one has eyes the color of the sky," said another.

"Wait until Neptu sees how healthy they are," said Fari. "He will be pleased. We have done well."

"Is Neptu as cruel as they say?" Kael asked. His stomach churned.

The room filled with laughter.

"We have heard that he rules the Big Water," Gonter said. "We were told to stay away from him."

"Oh, he rules the Big Water, all right," said Fari. "He rules all of us down here."

Kael frowned. "Down here? Where are we?"

Fari clucked her little tongue. "I already told you. You are in Neptu's home."

"And where is that?" asked Gonter.

She smiled. "At the bottom of the sea, of course."

Kael's jaw dropped.

"How did we get here?" Gonter asked.

Giggling filled the room again.

Fari hid a laugh behind her delicate little hand. "We brought you here. We are his helpers."

Kael's mouth went dry. "Can we go home again?"

Fari lifted her shoulders and let them drop. "Only Neptu can answer that."

"What are we going to do?" Kael whispered to Gonter.

"Ssh," warned Fari. "I hear him coming."

The sound of heavy steps headed their way.

"Where are you, my little ones?" The low, rumbling words rebounded off the walls. The colors in the room bounced as well, rearranging themselves in a clashing, flashing pattern.

Kael's knees shook. Loyal as always, Gonter stood right beside him.

"AHHHH-CHOOO!"

Kael grabbed hold of Gonter to keep from being blown over. His eyes rounded. Neptu had to be big if he had a sneeze like that.

"SNIFFLE, SNIFFLE."

The sound grew louder and louder. Kael drew in a deep breath. It came out in a little squeak when an enormous man entered the room.

Blue hair hung in ringlets around his head. His long beard matched the color of his hair and was as curly. Green eyes stared at the boys and then closed as another sneeze shook the room.

Kael and Gonter tumbled to the ground with the force of it.

"Sorry," said Neptu, holding out a hand to each of them. "This blasted cold continues to linger."

Neptu's hand was chilly to the touch and a little bit slimy. His clothing appeared to be woven together from the greens that grew in the water. His round belly was bare and had a tinge of blue, like the water.

"Come with me," said Neptu, easing himself into the steamy pool of warm water. "We can talk while I soak."

Fari and her friends buzzed around Neptu, brushing his hair, combing his beard, and singing.

Neptu leaned his head back and closed his eyes. “Ah-h-h! This feels good. I have been on a long tour of duty. Sit, boys, so we can talk.”

Kael and Gonter dutifully sat by the pool, dangling their feet in the warm water, until Kael could stand the suspense no longer. He cleared his throat. "Will you let us go back home? Fari said it was up to you."

Neptu opened his eyes and sat up. "Home? Now, why do you want to do that?"

Kael drew himself up. "Gonter and I are traveling to find my family. During a raid, my mother and sister were taken captive. We are to learn new things and share the information with others.”

"It is important. Wise men have spoken," added Gonter. “They have said it is how we all will survive in our changing world."

Neptu nodded thoughtfully. "Why did the boy in the boat leave you behind?"

Kael felt his eyes widen.

"You are shocked I know such things?" said Neptu. "I know many things about the Big Water and the people who use it. You need to prove to me that you are worthy of being returned to the world above. Come up with three good reasons why I should let you go."

Kael swallowed hard. He and Gonter huddled together.

"How should we answer?" said Gonter.

"The first one is easy," said Kael. He turned to Neptu. "We have already told you that we have been given a mission to share information with other clans in order for them to survive."

Neptu grunted and said nothing.

Gonter shuffled his feet and spoke. "We have left Maida and Brota behind. They are worried about us. If we do not continue our mission, Maida will not be able to continue hers. It will not be as Grandfather was told in a special dream."

“And the third reason?” Neptu asked.

Kael took a deep breath. He could not help the tears that filled his eyes.

“My father was the bravest hunter of our clan. He lost his life so that I and others could live. I want to be as brave and as good a man as he.” His voice caught. “I must find my mother and my little sister to make sure they are all right.”

Neptu let out another sneeze that rocked Kael and Gonter back on their heels. He stared at them with green eyes that seemed to reach inside each boy.

Kael held his breath.

"You have answered well,” Neptu said after anxious moments. “It is only right for me to have the little ones take you back. You will do good for others; that much I know. First, you must do something for me. It will be proof of your worthiness.”

“What?” Gonter asked eagerly.

“As you can see, I have a cold. It does not happen often, but when it does, it takes a long time for me to recover.” Neptu stopped talking and blew his nose into a wide piece of seaweed that Fari and his other helpers dangled in front of him.

"Yes... what do you want us to do?" Kael prompted Neptu anxiously.

"You know the storm that caught you by surprise?" Neptu continued, sniffling slightly. "Well, it was an accident. I did not mean to get so upset. Now I have to make certain that all who were caught in its path are all right. That is where I need your assistance."

Kael caught the corner of his lip. He was a good swimmer, but not that good.

Gonter's brow wrinkled. "Assist you? You are the one who rules the Big Water."

"Perhaps, perhaps not," said Neptu, shrugging. "Let us say I try my best to help all the creatures in or on the Big Water. Right now, I am worried about a young Spouter. I am afraid the storm might have thrown him on shore, away from his mother. I need you to make sure he is not trapped on land."

"And if he is, how could we free him? They are enormous," said Kael.

Neptu began to laugh. His belly moved up and down in the water, sending wave after wave racing to the edge of the pool. The sound of his laughter thundered against the cavern walls in steady beats.

Gonter, always full of questions, spoke boldly. "Please, tell us what we have to do. We want to go back to the world above, to Maida and Brota and our mission."

Neptu's eyes rounded. "Ah, I see how serious you are. You wonder how you can help? You must use your imagination. Think."

An idea struck Kael. "I know. Fari and her friends can help us. They have magical powers. After all, they brought us here."

Neptu nodded with satisfaction. "They will take you to the place where I noticed the Spouter. It will be up to you to figure out how to save it. Then, you will be free to go."

Fari flew over to Neptu and whispered in his ear. He listened and turned to the boys. "Fari is ready. Close your eyes and she will take you away from here. I will see you later, when your task is complete."

Kael's body hummed with excitement and more than a little fear. He sat where Fari indicated and closed his eyes. He felt Gonter's arm go around his shoulders and was comforted to know that no matter where Fari took them, they would be together.

Fari's voice trilled in front of them. "Sleep."

Her tiny hands brushed across Kael's eyelids, like the whisper of a gentle breeze, and darkness came.

CHAPTER ELEVEN

Maida paced the shore of the Big Water, glancing out to sea, again and again. Brota kept in step beside her. She carried two paddles. One had a whale carved at its end, the other a wolf. They had washed ashore earlier. Everyone agreed it was a troubling sign. Still, Maida would not give up on the idea that her friends would return. She gave one last glance at the rolling waves, let out a sigh, and went back to her home.

As she entered, her father said, "No sign of them?"

"Not yet," she answered. "Father, I am more certain than ever that Damo did not tell the whole truth about the accident. He will not look me in the eye when I try to talk to him about it. Please, Father, I beg you, ask the boys one more time what happened. It could help us find Kael and Gonter."

Hetar nodded. "Let me talk to Chief Vukon."

Later, the boys in the clan, along with Maida and her father, were called to the chief's home.

Chief Vukon eyed each boy carefully. "It has come to my attention that the accident in the storm might have happened differently from what was first reported." He glanced at his son. "As painful as it might be for any of us, the time has come to tell the truth. Two boys have been lost at sea. I demand to know what happened."

"I told you already," said Damo. He turned to the others.

The other boys remained quiet.

Gropa stepped forward. "Damo told us not to tell, but I cannot remain quiet any longer. Kael and Gonter were washed overboard by a big wave and were alive and swimming toward the boat when Damo ordered us to continue paddling." His face was awash with shame. "We did not try to save them."

Maida gasped and covered her mouth with her hands, her eyes filling with tears.

Chief Vukon's expression turned angry. He pointed a shaking finger at Damo. "You are no longer worthy to be a leader of the young hunters. Gropa will take your place. He and the others will go on the hunting trip to come. *You* will stay behind."

"He is lying!" In a fit of temper, Damo shoved Gropa.

"I am sorry, son. The truth always comes out in the end," said Chief Vukon, taking hold of Damo's arm. "We can pray that some miracle will happen, and Kael and Gonter will be returned to us." He shook his head. "That, however, is not likely to happen."

Maida fought back fresh tears. "No!" She could not let her people believe that Kael and Gonter were lost to them forever. "They *will* come back. You will see." Inside, her heart was breaking. She and Brota raced out of the house and down to the beach.

"We have to find them," she said to Brota.

She cupped her hands over her eyes, searching the water for them, and finally turned away, trying unsuccessfully to hold back fresh tears.

CHAPTER TWELVE

Kael felt the pull of receding waves tug on his body and opened his eyes. Beside him, Gonter lay on the edge of the sand, his face turned to the sky.

"We are back," said Kael, standing unsteadily. He spied a large, black shape farther down the shore and tugged on Gonter's arm. "Wake up! We are here, and the Spouter Neptu told us about is nearby."

Gonter's blue eyes flashed open. He sat up groggily.

Kael helped Gonter to his feet and studied the shoreline. "Neptu was right. The Spouter has washed too close to shore to get back into the water."

"How will we get it? It is huge!" Gonter said.

"That is what Neptu wanted us to figure out."

They trotted down the beach and

approached the Spouter with care.

Kael's gaze swept over the large creature. He recalled the wooden Spouter Parni had carved for him. He realized that though Parni had made its shape true to life, he had not been able to capture the enormous size of one. And Neptu had called this Spouter a baby.

The young Spouter's eyes followed their movement as they came closer. Eyes wide with panic, it flopped around in the shallow water.

"Do not worry," said Kael, wading to its side. "We are not going to hurt you. Neptu sent us."

"Yes," Gonter said, rubbing a gentle hand over the smooth skin. "We are going to help get you free."

"I have to get back into the water or I will die," the Spouter said in a deep voice.

Kael's eyes widened. "You talk?" Ronaldo, the wise man of his clan, had told Kael that he would meet animals that could talk, but it always surprised him.

"I usually talk only to Neptu and his helpers," the Spouter replied. Tears spilled out of its eyes and glistened on the dark skin of its body. “I need to find my mother.”

Kael thought of his own mother. Pain struck like a knife to his heart.

“We promised Neptu we would help you,” Kael said. “I have an idea.” He explained that with each wave that came ashore, they would use the pull of the receding water to help them push him back. It would be like Hetar’s men with their boat.

A wave splashed ashore. Gonter and Kael moved to the front of the Spouter and pushed as the wave pulled back.

The Spouter did not budge.

“Where are Fari and the others? We need help. The Spouter’s way too big for us to handle alone,” said Gonter. His breath came out in puffy gasps.

Kael tried to remain calm. The Spouter was beginning to appear as if it would not make it. Neptu had told them to use their imagination. Was it a trick of some kind?

He closed his eyes and concentrated his thoughts on the tiny girl. When he opened his eyes, a flickering light appeared in front of him. “Fari?”

Fari flew out of the light and smiled at him. “You wanted to see me?”

Kael nodded. “We need your help,” he told her solemnly. “This Spouter will die without it.”

“I see,” Fari’s high voice rang with concern. “Neptu would not like that. Let us see what we can do.” She clapped her hands together, and the twinkling lights that shimmered on the water rose up and gathered around her.

“Fairies,” she said sweetly, “these boys have asked for our help. It is time to work our magic. This Spouter will die without it.”

A chorus of dismay followed her words.

“We need to push the Spouter back into the water when the waves retreat,” Kael explained. “Gonter and I cannot do it alone.”

“Very well,” Fari said, and a whole cluster of the little fairies gathered at the nose of the Spouter.

Remembering the chant that Hetar used to get the men pushing and pulling together, Kael said, “When I say push, use your magic and push with all your strength.”

He began to chant, “Steady, steady, *push*!

Steady, steady, *push*!"

Slowly, gently, they eased the Spouter back into the water.

"We did it!" cried Gonter triumphantly.

The whale began to swim in circles in front of them.

"Thank you, Fari," said Kael. "You and your friends helped save him."

She shook her tiny head. "It was your willingness to believe in us that did it."

The Spouter playfully dipped below the surface and rose. A spray of water shot up in the air from the hole on the top of its head.

"Now I know why they call it a Spouter," Kael said, in awe of this beautiful creature.

"Are we free to go now?" Gonter asked Fari. "We did as Neptu asked."

The Spouter swam near them. "Where is my mother? How am I going to find her?"

"Neptu did not say anything about finding its mother. We have done the job he asked us to do," Gonter said.

Kael nodded, but he was troubled.

"We cannot leave him," Gonter said. "It

would not be right."

Kael shook his head. "No, it would not be right."

Gonter's shoulders slumped. "How are we going to find its mother?"

"Are you ready for me to take you back to your people?" Fari asked. "You have done as Neptu asked."

Kael shook his head reluctantly. "We cannot go yet. Not until we find the Spouter's mother."

"It would not be right to leave him now," said Gonter. "He is a baby."

Neptu rose from the water and walked toward them—a huge, bluish figure, dripping seaweed from his body, ruffling the waters as he moved. A smile creased his face.

"You have done well, my friends, very well, indeed. You have passed my test. It is one thing to say that you will help your clans to survive. It is another, to help different creatures everywhere. You were willing to stay and help the Spouter find its mother, even when you realized you had already done what I had asked." He placed a cold, blue hand on top of Kael's curls and another on Gonter’s sunny locks.

“I will see that the Spouter finds its mother, and I will take you back to where the girl and the wolf wait for you. First, let me tell you about a place where they need your help. It is in the Land of Whispering Trees, along the coast below us. It will be another adventure for you. Now, come with me.”

The sun had not yet risen when Maida was awakened by Brota's cold nose on her cheek.

"What is it, boy?" She sat up and rubbed her eyes.

Brota nudged her again with his nose and started for the hut’s entrance.

Maida's heart pounded. Brota was trying to tell her something. She clambered to her feet and followed him out of the house.

He led her down to the water's edge and began to trot away from the village. He followed the shoreline, nose in the air. The warm glow from the rising sun helped Maida find her footing in the dim light.

Brota let out a yip and began galloping ahead

of her. Maida raced as fast as she could to keep pace with him. Her feet pounded on the sand, one hopeful step after another.

Brota howled and threw himself into the water. Shocked, Maida gaped at the sight of the wolf riding the waves, heading out to sea. Brota had always been afraid of the water.

Two shapes rose out of the frothy surface. Maida stared and shouted with glee, "Kael! Gonter! I knew it! I knew it!"

She dashed into the Big Water to greet them.

Arm in arm, Kael and Gonter waded ashore, grinning broadly. Brota pranced by their side.

Maida gave them hugs. "Brota and I waited and waited for you. What happened? How did you get here? It is a miracle."

Kael and Gonter glanced at each other.

"We were in another magical place." Gonter's eyes sparkled.

Kael nodded. "*She* will believe us, even if no one else will. Maida, we are going to the Land of Whispering Trees!"

“Our friend, Neptu, told us that we can do some good for others there,” said Gonter. He placed a hand on her shoulder. "And we want you to go with us."

"Yes. It would not be the same without you," agreed Kael, accepting her hug.

Maida's happy smile ended in a giggle of delight.

Soon, all three of them would be in the Land of Whispering Trees.

CHAPTER THIRTEEN

Kael shifted from one foot to the other, eager to be on his way. Traveling had become a way of life. He glanced at Gonter, his brother-in-spirit, and at Maida, the girl who had saved their lives. He knew they were as excited as he was to begin their next adventure.

Chief Vukon drew the attention of the crowd gathered on the sand by the Big Water.

“We bid farewell to our visitors, Kael and Gonter, and to Maida of our clan,” said the chief. “We are proud of Maida’s ability to be a strong, capable, and kind companion, as our wise man dreamed. We have heard the story of how she saved these boys’ lives and how she helps them on their journey. The boys have told me that Maida is their sister-spirit and requested that she join them. We wish them a safe journey as they travel the world to find Kael’s family and to bring back new ideas to us and others. Learning new ways is how clans will grow wiser and survive longer."

Maida's father placed an arm around her and spoke to the crowd. "It is right, daughter, that you accompany Kael and Gonter. You showed us the same loyalty as your friend, Gonter, in not giving up your belief in their return. You share the same kind of bravery as your friend, Kael, in facing the criticism of others who have tried to belittle your skills. And always, your kind heart has pleased us. Now, it is your turn to do as you wish and accompany the boys on this journey. Grandfather has trained you well, and the boys are trustworthy." He placed one hand on Kael's shoulder, another on Gonter's. "Travel well, young friends."

Kael waved goodbye to Maida's people.

Brota, Gonter's pet wolf, ran ahead of them, yipping.

As the only member of his clan to escape a raid on his village, Kael had been left alone. He had set out in his world, hoping to find his mother and his little sister, who had been taken captive. Now, he followed his friends along the shoreline of the Big Water toward warmer lands.

Brota splashed in and out of the water, racing back and forth on the sandy beach.

Kael dipped his feet in the cool waves at the shore's edge. The Big Water was an endless blue color.

As they hiked, the temperature changed from cool to warm to hot. Soon, heat filled the air and stole Kael's breath. The sun beat down on his tan skin.

Gonter's fair skin turned pink. He waved them over to the tall fir trees that bordered the shore.

Under the shade of the trees, Kael sipped water and lay on the ground beside his friends. When they had cooled enough to continue, they stayed close to the tree line, hiding in the shade, moving as fast as they could.

At the sound of a branch snapping behind him, Kael raised his spear and whipped around. He barely breathed as he listened to another sound like it. All he heard was the chirping of birds and the pounding of waves on the sand.

"What's wrong?" Gonter's eyes, the color of

the sky, were filled with worry.

Kael shrugged. "I am not sure."

"We need to take a rest," said Maida, wiping the sweat from her brown face. She sank to the ground. Reaching into her leather carrying sac, she pulled out a strip of leather and tied her long, black hair behind her head.

Panting from the heat, Brota lay between Gonter and Kael.

Kael opened his leather sac and pulled out the dried fish and pine nuts Maida's mother had given them. They eagerly dug into the food, sharing equally, leaving some for Brota.

Kael took a swig of water and leaned against the trunk of a tree.

Maida spread out on the crinkly, dry grass beneath the trees and closed her eyes.

Gonter and Brota fell asleep nearby.

As he dozed, images of his destroyed village played in Kael's mind. Following his mother's orders, he had run into the forest, away from the raiders. He had returned to find the village's mud and stick huts crushed to the ground. Wooden bowls, fur clothing, cooking skins, and other personal items were scattered all around. Everyone was gone except for Ronoldo, the clan's wise man, who lay dying from a wound to his side.

A voice in Kael's head suddenly screamed a warning. His eyes flashed open. He sat up.

A figure rushed toward him.

"Watch out!" Kael screamed. He scrambled to his feet and grabbed his spear.

Brota charged the figure, knocking him to the ground.

Gonter threw himself on top of the attacker, and a fierce struggle began.

An axe caught Kael's attention. He aimed his spear at the hand holding it, and the axe fell to the ground.

Maida snatched it up and stood nearby, ready to use it.

Gonter pinned the attacker down on the ground and sat back on his heels, breathing hard.

"Damo!" Maida cried. "What are you doing here? You should be back with our people."

Damo struggled beneath Gonter's firm grip.

"It is *your* fault, Maida! *I* should be traveling with these boys, not *you*!"

Kael held his spear over Damo. "You were not chosen to explore because you hurt others to get your way. You proved that by leaving Gonter and me in the Big Water to drown. We would never travel with you."

Gonter stood by, ready to seize him again.

Damo glared at them, rubbing his hand where Kael's spear had struck.

"What should we do with him?" Gonter asked the other two. “He is *not* coming with us.”

"We will keep the axe and send him back to his clan,” Kael said. “Without a weapon, he would be foolish to follow us any farther. Even he knows that."

"Yes," agreed Maida. "And unless he gets back to them in a hurry, they will find out he left without permission. And if that happens, Chief Vukon will make his life miserable.”

Damo sat on the ground. "I want to be the leader of the young hunters in our clan," he whined.

Maida let out a sigh of exasperation. "You

and I grew up together, and you have not changed one bit. You do not understand that to become a leader, one must listen to others, be willing to help them, and want the best for each one. Go back to our people, Damo, and speak to my grandfather. Perhaps he will give you wisdom. You do not seem to have any of your own."

"Yes," said Gonter. "Leave now."

Damo grinned at Maida. "Your grandfather is the wisest man in our clan. He trained you for all this. In time, he might do the same for me."

He rose to his feet and turned to Kael and Gonter. "I will go now, but someday, I will travel the world like the three of you. You cannot stop me. As the chief's son, I will order Maida's grandfather to give me all of his secrets. Then, I will be the leader, and everyone will obey *me*."

Disgust crossed Maida's face. "You never learn. Even now, you will not listen. Leave now."

Kael watched Damo trot away, relieved to see the last of him. Damo was twisted, like Borlan, the older boy in his own clan, who had laid a curse upon him. A curse that Gonter and Maida knew nothing about. A curse that Kael silently vowed to overcome, so his friends would be safe.

The sun sank below the horizon, giving them relief from the heat. They rolled out their furs and lay at the edge of the beach. The sound of the waves tapping the shore and rolling back into the sea soothed Kael. He inhaled the salty air, lay on his back, and glanced up at the sky. The lights there winked at him.

"I wonder where those lights came from," he said in a sleepy voice.

"People in my clan make shapes of them," said Maida. “Not even Grandfather knows why they are there.”

"What makes them shine?" persisted Kael, puzzled as always by the world around him. Not even the wise man of his clan could answer the questions Kael had always had about their mysterious surroundings.

As the others slept, Kael lay quietly. He clasped the claw necklace his mother had given him. His father had worn it when he had stayed behind to fight a Growler so that others could flee to safety.

Kael had been told he had the gift of bravery, but he knew he would never be as brave as his father. Even now, an image of a growling bear attacking his father made Kael's stomach knot and his eyes sting.

Curling his fingers into fists, Kael promised to find his mother and sister, who had been taken captive.

The landscape changed as they left the Big Water. No longer did the tall evergreen trees of the forest push their way onto the beaches. The trees now had thick, brown trunks and wide, shiny, green leaves.

They entered the interior. The foliage became a jungle. Long, creeping vines covered pathways and spread along the ground amid tall trees and thick undergrowth. In places, they had to cut their way through the greenery with a knife and an axe. By the time the sun began to sink, they were exhausted.

"We need to find a place to sleep." Maida kicked at the vines on the ground with a leather-covered foot.

Kael pulled out the axe that Comer, the wood carver in Maida's clan, had given him. Gonter used Damo's axe. They cleared a wide circle in the underbrush.

Maida built a fire in the middle of the clearing to keep wild animals away. They placed bunches of cut vines underneath their furs for soft sleeping places.

Maida searched through her carrying sac and lifted out a skin-wrapped package. Smiling, she showed them the large, pink fishcake inside.

Kael eagerly accepted food from her and bit into a small piece. Delicious. His travels had taught him that each clan prepared different foods, using what they could find from the land and water around them. People in all clans enjoyed tasty food.

They ate quietly, stoked the fire, and settled down, too tired to stay awake.

The sun was little more than a pale yellow light in the gray sky when Kael opened his eyes and wiped a raindrop from his face. He sat up and moved his furs under a nearby tree, calling softly to Gonter and Maida.

Brota joined the three of them beneath the broad leaves of a wide tree at the edge of the circle they had cleared. The rain poured from the sky. Water ran off the leaves above them and hit the ground with a steady beat.

Kael held out his skin water sac.

"I will fill mine too," said Gonter.

Soon, all their water sacs were full.

Kael reached up and tugged on a huge leaf. It came loose in his hands. Grinning, he placed it over his head and stepped out into the rain. Dry beneath the huge leaf, he pranced in the rain.

Gonter and Maida each grabbed a giant leaf and stepped into the circle, laughing and dancing with Kael.

Brota barked and joined them, standing on his hind legs in a dance of his own.

The rain stopped as suddenly as it had started, and the air became hot and heavy. Eager to be on their way among the whispering trees they had been told about, they ate a cold meal of dried berries.

The greenery remained thick. Vines crept up trees, covering their bark with a winding trail of leaves. Calls from birds sang out from time to time.

Clutching his spear, Kael listened for any sounds of larger animals. There were no disturbing roars or growls.

As they continued on their way, it grew quiet. Too quiet. The movement of the long branches hanging from the tops of the tall trees rustled back and forth, whispering danger.

The hair on the back of Kael's neck stood up. Something was nearby. Every nerve ending told him so.

Ping! Something hit him on the top of his head. Kael glanced around and picked up a good-sized nut.

Ping! It happened again. Kael looked up.

A brown, furry animal with a long, curling tail sat in the tree above them. Its mouth spread in a wide, toothy grin. Suddenly, many brown, furry faces peered down at them.

Gonter gathered Brota close and stayed right next to Kael and Maida.

Shrill laughter filled the air, so loud that Kael and the others were forced to cover their ears.

One of them swung down from the tree and landed on its feet. His long tail curled in a loop behind him. He poked a finger in the middle of Kael's chest.

"Who are you? Where are you from? Who are your friends? Huh?"

Kael was not surprised by the animal's ability to speak. Ronoldo, the wise man of his clan, had told him he would meet animals who could talk. He had already met quite a few. "I am Kael, from the Clan of the Forest."

The odd animal glanced at Gonter. "We have never seen one such as you. Your hair and your eyes..." He gave Gonter's sunny locks a tug. "Where do you come from?"

"The Clan of the Mountain. I am Gonter."

The creature turned to Maida.

"My name is Maida. I am from the Land of Fire and Ice. Who are you?"

He scratched his head. "What are you travelers doing here?"

"We are searching for the Land of the

Whispering Trees," Gonter replied. "We were told to come here."

"I am searching for my family," said Kael.

"We are traveling the world to learn new things," said Gonter.

"For the survival of our people," Maida added.

"Survival, huh?" he chuckled. "Take it from me, Kee, you will have to fight to survive here."

Kee's friends began to chatter with excitement.

"I believe we are in the Land of the Whispering Trees." Kael wondered why Neptu had wanted them to come to this strange place.

"Yes, indeed, you are here," replied Kee. "Kongo will be pleased to see you."

"Who is Kongo?" Maida asked.

"He is the leader of us Chatters, that is who. He was hoping some travelers would come to our land." His smile grew sly. "I do believe you are exactly what we have been hoping for."

Kael's mouth went dry. He did not like the sound of things or the way Kee was smiling at him. "Run!" he shouted.

Brown bodies swung down together from the trees. One grabbed hold of Maida. Another captured Gonter. Kael felt hands on his shoulder and turned to fight, but he was outnumbered.

Kee shook a finger at them. "You will never escape with all these vines and undergrowth blocking your way. You must stay with us. Kongo needs you."

"He is your leader, you say?" said Gonter, shaking off one of the strange animals. "What does he want with us?"

"You will see." Kee turned to his friends. "All right, Chatters, it will take two of us to carry each one of them. Four of you better handle that wolf. The rest of you can carry their things."

Kee took hold of Maida's arm.

She jerked it away. "What are you going to do with us?"

Kee seemed surprised. "Why, we are taking you to Kongo." He and another animal lifted her up into a tree.

Gonter and Brota followed. Then, it was Kael's turn.

Swoop, swing, swoop! Swoop, swing, swoop!

The ground beneath Kael became a blur as the two Chatters carrying him swung from one tree to another.

Kael caught a glimpse of Gonter and Maida ahead of him. In the safety of the Chatters' arms, they looped up in the air and swooped back down again. Howling from time to time, Brota hung limp in the air.

The chattering of these unusual animals was often interrupted by laughter. They seemed like a happy, friendly group. The lump of worry in Kael's throat grew smaller.

Kee called a halt to their travels.

The Chatters lowered Kael to the ground beside his friends and lay back against the trunks of trees. They folded their long, thin arms behind their heads.

Kael sat on the ground, grateful for its firmness beneath him. He rubbed his sore shoulders. Being carried through the trees was not as easy as it might seem.

Gonter shook his head. "How will we ever find our way out of this land?"

Kael lifted his hands helplessly. The view

from the treetops confirmed that the thick jungle would be nearly impossible to travel through on the ground.

Kee strolled over to them, holding a yellow oblong object. He peeled back the covering, revealing something white inside. He handed it to Kael.

Kael stared at it. “What is it?”

“A treat,” said Kee. “Go ahead. Take a bite. You will like it.”

Kael ate a small piece. It was a little sweet, a little mushy. He took another bite.

"I told you that you would like it," said Kee.

Kael nodded. "Where did you get it?"

Kee pointed to a tall green stalk in their midst, loaded with a long bunch of the odd-looking fruit.

"What do you call it?" Gonter asked.

"Pana," said Kee.

Kael handed the pana over to Gonter, who took a bite and handed it to Maida.

Kee handed each of them another pana. “We will rest here until the worst of the heat has passed.”

Kael leaned back against the trunk of a tall tree, enjoying each bite of the unusual food.

Kee and his friends rested nearby, silent now.

Brota stopped his restless pacing and lay down beside Gonter.

Maida curled up under a tree for a nap.

Kael's eyes closed.

CHAPTER FOURTEEN

The singsong calls of birds stirring in the trees above them signaled the end of their rest.

Kee appeared at Kael's side. "We must keep going or Kongo will wonder where we are. He does not like to be kept waiting."

The Chatters lifted them into the trees, then they took off.

When the Chatters finally swung down to the ground, the setting sun was spreading rosy color in the darkening sky.

Kael swayed on his feet, trying to get used to the firm surface beneath him.

The sound of someone crashing through the underbrush stopped any talk among them.

Kee and his fellow Chatters lined up and stood at attention.

A large, furred animal, as wide and tall as a Growler, marched toward them on two feet. He had the same dark eyes and button nose as Kee, except no friendly smile appeared on his round face.

The fur on Brota's back rose.

Kael, Maida, and Gonter moved closer to each other.

"These are the only visitors you could find?" the large beast asked. "What is that...that Howler doing here? I told you what I wanted." He pounded his fists on his broad chest one after the other.

"I know, I know," apologized Kee. "They will do. They are strong. You will see." He tugged on Gonter's arm, dragging him forward. "Tell Kongo your name."

"I am Gonter from the Clan of the Mountains, and this is my pet, Brota."

Kongo pointed at Maida. "She is with you? A girl?"

Maida stepped forward, her back straight. "I am as skilled as any boy. My grandfather taught me to hunt and fish."

"Her name is Maida. I am Kael, from the Clan of the Forest." Kael tried to match Kongo's bold stare but turned away.

"We cannot stay here," said Gonter. "We must keep searching for Kael's family."

Kongo waved a long finger at him. "We must see how the war ends before anyone leaves."

Gonter's face fell. "War? What war?"

Kongo turned to Kee. "They do not know about Alli?"

Kee ducked his head. "I figured it was best to get them here first."

Kael's body turned cold. "What's going on, Kee?"

"You did not tell us anything about a war," said Gonter.

"You!" roared Kongo, pointing to Gonter. "Be quiet and listen to me. We are at war, and you are on our side."

"What are you fighting about?" Gonter said.

Kongo pointed to a small pond in the distance. "Alli will not let us go into the water, so we will not let him come on our land."

Kael's stomach twisted with worry. "Who is Alli?" He had heard horrible stories about a war between his own clan and another in an earlier time.

"Alli? He is a strange one—ugly, really ugly, all green and scaly," Kongo said. "He and his group are nothing like us. You will see for yourself." He wrinkled his nose with distaste.

"Right," said Kee, nodding up and down. "Those Scalees should not be allowed to share land with the likes of us. We are way too good for them." The other Chatters murmured their agreement.

Kael glanced at Gonter with dismay. It sounded as if this battle had been going on for some time.

Kongo marched over and jabbed a finger at Kael. "We have to teach them a lesson. *I am* the king of the jungle, not Alli. This land is *ours*."

"Land without access to water does not work. Everyone needs water to live," said Gonter.

"Of course. That is why we want them to give us rights to the water. In return, they want to use our land. We do not want those ugly Scalees living among us. The only way to solve this is to declare war and take over the pond."

"That's not fair," said Gonter.

Maida's dark eyes flashed with anger. "You have no right to keep us prisoners.”

"Keep quiet. I am the king of the jungle, nobody else.” Kongo pounded his foot in a fit of temper, exactly like Kael’s little sister used to do when she did not get her way. “Kee! Take him away."

Maida’s dark eyes flashed with anger. “You have no right... ”

“Take her too,” bellowed Kongo.

Sending Kael a look of regret, Kee took Maida’s arm and led her away.

Others followed with Gonter and Brota.

When Kael turned to follow them, Kongo placed a firm hand atop Kael’s curls.

"You outsiders think you know how things should be. You do not.” Kongo let out an angry puff of breath. “We must win this battle, even if it means a few die.”

Die? Alarm shot through Kael. "I do not want to be part of a war. Why not talk to each other?"

“Take him away with the others," Kongo roared.

Hands gripped Kael painfully. It was confusing. They had been told to come to the Land of Whispering Trees to help others. Now, they were trapped.

The Chatters dragged Kael to a small hut whose walls were made of stacked logs bound together with vines. The roof consisted of thin branches woven together and covered with broad leaves, like the ones they had danced with in the rain not long ago.

One of the Chatters shoved Kael through the hut's entrance. He caught his balance and stood inside, trying to see in the dim light.

Gonter and Maida greeted him, worried.

The three of them gathered close.

"We have to come up with a way to get out of here," said Gonter.

"Kongo is crazy," said Maida. "Kee told me things were disorganized before Kongo took over. Now, he and the other Chatters follow Kongo's orders. They think it will make life happier."

"Happier? They spend their time fighting,"

said Kael.

"What do you think is going to happen to us?" asked Maida.

"We will find out soon enough." Kael could not hold back the worry he always carried with him. Was Borlan's curse the reason things had gone so wrong?

Darkness came. Kael tossed and turned on his furs inside the hut. Each time one of the Chatters peered inside, Brota let out a growl. No one slept.

It was early when Kael walked outside the hut with Maida and Gonter.

Kee hurried over to them. "Stay here. We will bring you water. You cannot go down to the pond."

Kael nodded and waited for Kee to return. Gonter and Maida stood talking quietly to one side, keeping an eye on Brota. The wolf circled the area, sniffing the air.

A high-pitched shriek shattered the quiet.

The Chatters cried out and ran toward the pond.

Kael ran after them.

Maida, Gonter, and Brota followed.

Screeching in outrage, the Chatters gathered at the edge of the pond.

Kael pushed his way through the crowd to get see better. A scaly green swimmer held a small Chatter in its long jaw.

The Chatters threw stones and pieces of wood at the water enemy.

Kongo appeared, towering over the others. "That is enough, Alli. We have hostages now. Return the Chatter to me, and I will let you have one of them in exchange. The hostages will make a better meal than that skinny little Chatter."

The gator-like figure moved closer to shore. His dark eyes gleamed as his gaze swept over Kael, Maida, and Gonter and came to rest on Brota. He opened his jaw.

Sobbing, the freed Chatter hurried through the water to his mother's open arms.

"Now, give me one of those hostages," said Alli.

Kongo pointed to Maida. "You. Go to him. You are his now."

Kael moved closer to her. "She does not go alone."

Proving his gift of loyalty, Gonter stepped to the other side of her.

Before anybody could stop them, Kael and Gonter locked arms with Maida and raced into the pond.

Brota escaped the hold of one of the Chatters and followed.

A howl of protest rose from the Chatters.

“No fair!” Kongo screamed from the edge of the pond. "You cannot do that. You are *my* hostages, not *his*!"

"We are no one's hostages!" Gonter shouted back.

Alli floated in the water near them. A hideous grin opened his long jaw, making his mouth seem even larger. Fear numbed Kael’s body. He could not begin to count the number of sharp teeth that lined that jaw.

"You are mine," said Alli in a deep, gravelly voice. "Mine."

"No." Maida stood waist-deep in the water. "I will not belong to you or anyone else."

Alli's eyes bulged. He let out a raspy laugh. "Oh, we have a scrappy one here. Let us see how long that lasts. Come with me."

Kael glanced back at the Chatters on shore. With Kongo, there was no discussion, no freedom. He moved forward with Maida and Gonter.

Alli led them across the shallow pond. At the far end, a number of green Scalees crowded together in the tall grass, sunning themselves.

“See?” Gonter said. “They are lying on land here, and nobody is bothering them.”

“Then why fight?” Kael said.

"Maybe we will not have to be hostages, after all," said Maida.

Alli whirled around. His long tail swished behind him with a splash. "The war with Kongo is not over. Not until we Scalees win control of all the land."

Kael could not hold back. "Why fight if it’s not necessary?"

Alli ignored him and continued swimming. He called to the others on land. “See what I have.”

The Scalees, who had been sleeping in the sun, entered the water on short legs and easily surrounded them.

Alli greeted them with a wide smile. "See? Hostages from Kongo!"

One after another, tooth-filled snouts opened to laugh.

Kael gripped Maida's hand and nodded to Gonter.

Chins held high, they waded through the swimming creatures and walked onto land.

One of the Scalees on shore eyed Brota with hunger.

"I would not try anything," Gonter warned him. "Brota can be vicious."

A small gator-like wild thing let out a raspy chuckle. "Your wolf would make a nice snack for Alli and some of the others."

"Not you, little Gader. You have a long way to grow before you could get your mouth around an animal like that," said one of the larger ones who had gathered round them.

Cough-like laughs erupted throughout the group.

The little one called Gader laughed with the rest of them. "I am going to be as big as the rest of you.”

"Not in my lifetime," smiled an elderly Scalee. He nudged Gader with his snout. "You have got a lot of spunk. I will say that about you."

Alli crept ashore. "Like I said," he announced to the group, "these are hostages from Kongo. I traded one of the Chatters for all three of these youngsters and their pet." He let out a grating laugh. "Kongo said it was not fair. He forgets we are at war."

Toothy snouts nodded up and down.

Kael’s heart sank. These Scalees were as stubborn as the Chatters. “We cannot stay here. As my friends and I are traveling the world to find my family, we are learning from others.”

"Our war council will meet to discuss exactly how you can help us,” said Alli. “Until then, do not attempt to leave. You would regret it." He snapped his jaw shut with a bone-rattling warning.

Kael swallowed hard and lowered himself to the ground.

Gonter sat beside Kael, holding onto Brota. Maida joined them.

Gader approached them with an eager gait. "You are really traveling the world? I wish I could see something other than this side of the pond." His voice grew wistful. "I suppose I never will."

"You have not been to the other side of the pond?" Gonter asked.

Gader shook his head. "There are all sorts of strange, evil animals over there. They are ugly and cruel. We are not supposed to get near them."

"Have you ever seen one?" Kael asked.

"Of course not," said Gader.

Maida shook her head. "Then how do you know what they are like?"

"Alli told us all about them."

"I thought you wanted to see the world for yourself," said Gonter. "Like the other side of the pond."

Gader's eyes bulged. "How...how would I do that?"

Kael beckoned Gader closer. "When it gets

dark, we will help you."

Gader's expression brightened. "You would come with me?"

"Yes. We need to pick up our belongings," said Kael.

"What about Alli? You are his hostages. You cannot leave." He shook his head. "No, that will not work."

"How about if we return to this side of the pond with you?" said Gonter.

Gader's long mouth opened in a wide grin. "Then I will have something to tell the other Scalees. For once, they might stop teasing me."

"Remember, Gader," warned Kael, "it is our secret. Do not mention this to anyone else."

Gader bobbed his head and crept away.

CHAPTER FIFTEEN

Darkness was a long time in coming. Lying on soft grass, Kael flipped from one side to the other. His eyes were beginning to close when he felt something cold and rough on his cheek. He swiped it away.

"Ow!" whispered Gader, rubbing his snout. "It is me. Ready to go?"

Kael bolted upright, poked Gonter and Maida, and checked the area.

Scattered groups of Scalees snuggled together in the tall grass away from the water. All was quiet except for the soft, steady sound of snoring.

Kael, Gonter, and Maida tiptoed to the water's edge and stepped in. In the hot, humid air, the cool water felt refreshing. Gader entered behind them. Step by cautious step, they silently moved toward the far side of the pond.

Kael nudged Gader. “Hurry.”

Gader slid onto the shore and lay still. Gonter and Brota hurried onto land and crouched beside him.

Following their plan, Maida and Kael crept past them and headed into the trees.

In the dark-time breeze, the leaves rustled on the trees, making a warning whisper.

A shiver crept across Kael’s shoulders. He tiptoed through the jungle growth beside Maida.

The small hut where they had been held captive lay ahead of them. Maida crept toward it while Kael hunkered down in the dark, keeping guard. One wrong move, and they would all be caught.

Suddenly, long fingers wrapped around Kael's throat, choking him. "What are you doing here alone?" Kee whispered in his ear.

"I need to get my belongings," Kael managed to say, frantically searching for Maida. She was nowhere to be seen.

"You are not going anywhere," Kee gasped, then crumpled to the ground and lay still.

“I have him.” Maida shot Kael a triumphant

grin and held up the large stick she had used to hit Kee on the head.

"Get Gonter to help me," whispered Kael. "He and I will carry Kee out of here."

Loaded down with their things, Maida took off.

Kael wrapped his arms around Kee and tugged. Trying not to make any noise, he dragged Kee's body over the rough ground.

Kee let out a low moan.

Heart pounding with fear, Kael covered Kee's mouth and scanned the trees. The sleeping shapes of Chatters remained still.

Gonter silently appeared beside Kael.

Moving as fast as they could, they carried Kee through the greenery.

Gader and Maida stood in the water, loaded down with their things.

Kael eased into the water's coolness and held Kee's head afloat, keeping an anxious eye on him so he would not wake up and call for help.

They moved through the water slowly, cautiously.

Gonter and Maida held furs and sacs above

their heads. Brota and Gader carried water sacs in their teeth. Kael checked Kee, still from the blow to the head. They would be back on firm ground after a few more steps.

Brota ran out of the pond and shook water off his fur coat.

Maida, Gonter, and Gader followed, unloading their gear in a heap.

Kael let out a sigh of relief when he felt solid, dry ground beneath his feet. He lowered Kee to the grass and stood over him.

Gader's eyes shone with excitement. "Hey, everybody, see who is here!"

A sea of green, scaly figures instantly surrounded them.

"What have you done?" roared Alli.

"We have captured a Chatter," said Gader proudly. "I helped."

Alli shook a claw at him. "You disobeyed me. You left our side of the pond."

"We wanted to get our belongings," explained Gonter. "This may turn out to be a benefit for you."

There was no mistaking Alli's anger. "This is

war! We do not have anything to do with the enemy!"

Kael took a deep breath and said, "At least give it a try."

“Chatters and Scalees do not mix,” said Alli. He poked Kee in the belly with his long snout.

Kee’s eyes opened. He blinked rapidly, let out a yowl, and leapt to his feet. “What am I doing here? Do not hurt me. I did nothing wrong.” His gaze fastened on Kael. “It is your fault. Tell them.”

Kael held up his hands. “It is all right. Nobody is going to hurt you.” He turned to Alli. “Allow Kee stay here with your group.”

A mother pushed her baby behind her. “No Chatter is going to touch any young one of mine!”

Her children said, “Why? What did he do?”

“Why?” his mother said, her voice shaking. “He is not one of us. Look at him! He has a round, furry face, long, skinny arms, lots of toes, and a curly tail.”

“Notice the three of us.” Kael said, indicating Maida and Gonter at his side. “We are all different, but we are the best of friends. Gonter is my brother-in-spirit, and Maida is like a sister to us. Yet, we are nothing alike." It was true. Gonter, with his pale skin, light hair, and eyes the color of the sky, was different from his spirit brother. Shorter, Kael had broader shoulders, tan skin, brown eyes, and dark curls. Maida was not a match to either one of them, not with her small, thin body, dark brown skin, black eyes, and straight black hair.

In the shocked quiet that followed, Maida stepped over to Kee and patted him on the head.

"Kee's brown fur is soft and silky. He uses his tail to travel through the trees." She waved Gader over. "Go ahead, feel how soft the fur is."

Gader's jaw dropped. He glanced around at the others, his eyes as wide as Kee's. He had wanted to *see* a Chatter, not *touch* one!

Kael gave Gader a little push.

Kee stood stiffly and closed his eyes.

Gader reached out with a shaking claw, touched a hair or two on the top of Kee's head, and withdrew it.

"Better try again, to show your friends how

brave you are," whispered Maida.

Gader gulped fresh air and lifted a claw.

Kee backed away.

Gader moved closer and lightly ruffled the fur on top of Kee's head. A smile of sorts lit his green, scaly face. He turned to the others. "It is soft, like she said."

Some of Gader's friends rushed over.

"I want to touch it," one cried.

"I want to ask him some questions," said another.

Kee shriveled into a ball and held his hands over his head.

Kael stepped forward. "Kee is afraid. Later, there will be time for everyone to talk to him to get to know him."

"Right," said Alli. "The sun is rising. It is time for everyone to go about their own business. Remember, we are still at war."

"I want to go back to my own kind," said Kee. He tugged on Kael's hand. "Why did you do this to me?"

"Of all the Chatters, you seemed more open to new ideas. I am glad it was you who discovered me in the jungle. This might change things.”

Gonter gave Kee a sympathetic pat on the back. "Having you here among these Scalees will be better for everyone."

They kept Kee close to them.

Over the next several sunrises, one Scalee after another approached Kee. At first, nothing more than a few words were spoken or silent gestures were made. Gradually, complete thoughts were exchanged.

The moment finally came when Kael heard comfortable laughter between Alli and Kee. He gave Maida a satisfied smile. Their plan was working.

Kee chattered and swung from a tree above their campsite. Gader and his friends stood below, watching him. Kee swooped down and grabbed one of the smallest Scalees, lifting the surprised young one high up into the air.

"Put my baby down. Right now!" his mother screamed, rising on her hind legs.

"No, Mama!" the youngster cried from Kee's

arms. "I am flying!"

Alli approached the mother. "It is all right. Kee is not going to hurt him. He is only showing us what he can do with his tail. Later, we are going to show him how we use our tails to swim."

As it grew dark, Kael gathered Gonter and Maida close. "I heard Alli talking to Kee. He wants to send Gader over to the other side of the pond with Kee. He is hoping to end the war. Our plan is working. It is time to leave."

"The circle of light will help show us the way out of here." Maida pointed to the glowing globe in the sky.

"After everyone is asleep, we will go," agreed Gonter.

They began to quietly pack their things.

Kael picked up his leather sacs and furs and waited for Gonter and Maida to do the same. Moving quietly, they crept away from the cluster of snoring Scalees.

He felt a prickle at the back of his neck and whipped around. Alli lay on the ground, one eye trained on him.

Kael froze, waiting nervously for Alli to respond. Gonter and Maida stopped beside him.

A toothy grin spread below Alli's watchful eyes. Silently, he lifted a claw in farewell.

Kael's breath came out in a grateful whoosh of air. "Thank you, Alli."

They moved once more through the thick undergrowth, careful to avoid fallen branches that could snap underfoot or vines that might cling to them.

Brota ran ahead, nose to the ground.

They had not gone far when Kael heard a noise in the trees above him and looked up. Kee leaped down from a tree, landing on top of him, shoving him to the ground.

Kee glared at Kael and turned to Gonter and Maida with a fierce frown. "Where are you going?"

Kael brushed Kee aside and pushed himself to his feet. "It is time for us to leave."

"I want you to stay," whined Kee. He sat and wrapped his arms around Kael's knees. "Do not leave. I am going to take Gader across the pond. We will not be at war anymore."

"That proves our point. There is really no need for us to stay any longer," said Kael. “We must continue our journey.”

"We need to be on our way,” said Gonter.

Maida gave Kee a gentle pat on the head. “Farewell.”

Kee's features crumpled. A huge teardrop rolled down his cheek. "I will always remember you. All of you."

His tears flowing freely now, Kee stood and wrapped his long, thin arms around each of them. Then, with one backward glance, he scrambled up a tree and swung away from them. Swoop, swing, swoop.

In the quiet that followed, the fronds of the trees rustled, as if to whisper, "*Farewell! Farewell!*"

CHAPTER SIXTEEN

They continued making their way through the undergrowth, eager to get as far away from the Land of Whispering Trees as possible. Alli had allowed them to leave, but the rest of the group might not be so willing. They had become used to having the three of them around.

The circle of light above them spread a glow over the landscape and helped them to see. They did not stop to rest until the early gray sky was painted with the pink promise of a new sunrise.

In a clearing, Kael stretched out on the ground, resting his head on a skin sac. Maida, Gonter, and Brota lay beside him.

They slept until Brota's growl brought them to their feet.

Gonter grabbed onto the fur at Brota's neck. "What is it, boy?"

Sniffing the air, Brota continued to growl.

Kael held up his hand. "Sssh! I hear something."

"Someone is crying," whispered Maida.

Gonter let go of Brota. "Easy, boy. Be gentle."

They followed Brota through the undergrowth.

The banks of a wide river appeared in front of them. A broad, flat boat rested on land. A young boy sat inside it. When he saw Brota, he jumped to his feet.

"Do not let him hurt me!" As he scrambled inside the boat, his long, dark, straight hair swung back and forth beneath a red band tied around his head.

Gonter called Brota back to his side. "It is all right," he said to the boy. "He will not hurt you."

"Who are you?" asked Maida.

"And what are you doing here all by yourself?" said Kael.

Fresh tears ran down the boy's cheeks. He climbed out of the boat and stood before them. "I am Sukey. I am from the People of the Rippling Waters." He hiccupped through his tears. "Or I *was*."

"What happened?" Maida asked gently. She squatted next to him and took hold of one of his hands.

Sukey caught his breath. "I ran away from home."

A kind heart was Maida's gift. She put her arm around him. "Tell us what happened."

Sukey's lower lip stuck out in a pout. "My baby sister, Neeno, was born."

Kael hid a smile. He remembered well the day his sister Rarey was born. He had felt a lot of jealousy, more than he thought he had.

"So, after she was born, you decided to leave?" Gonter asked.

Sukey shook his head. "Not right away. It was my brother Mikko. He called me the baby of the family because I cried. Then everybody teased me about being so small."

"And now that you are away from them?" Kael said.

Sukey blinked back tears. "I want to go home."

Kael gave him a pat on the back. He knew exactly how the little boy felt. Only he had no home to go back to. "We will help you get there."

A bright smile changed the little boy's face. His dark eyes sparkled.

Brota approached. Sukey held out his hand to the wolf, then laughed out loud when Brota licked the tears off his cheek.

Kael studied the boat. "Why is it so flat and wide?"

"The water is not deep, so we make our boats like this," replied Sukey. "We use a long pole to push it from place to place. I will show you how."

They climbed into the dugout, carefully arranging their packs for balance.

"Come, Brota." Gonter grabbed hold of the wolf and forced him into the boat. His body shaking, Brota crouched at Gonter's feet, rolling his eyes.

"He is afraid?" Sukey asked.

Gonter nodded. "He has never been in a boat before."

"I am not afraid. My people have always lived on the water," said Sukey with pride.

"How far is it to your home?" asked Maida. She cupped a hand over her eyes and scanned the horizon. "I see nothing but waving grass in the water."

Sukey grinned. "We are there. When we get closer, you will see." He stood at the stern of the boat and placed one end of a long pole in the water. He held onto the other end and pushed. As it shot forward, the water rippled away from the sides of the boat.

Push after push, they traveled through the wetlands. The boat stopped moving forward and slid back as Sukey fought the push of the wind.

"I can help," said Kael.

Taking Sukey's place at the stern, he lifted the pole, surprised to discover how light it was. He placed one end of the pole in the water and gave a mighty push. The boat surged ahead. Kael did not. With a splashing sound, he stood waist deep in the water.

Sukey laughed. "You forgot to lift the pole."

Feeling foolish, Kael waded toward the moving boat.

"Watch out for the snake," warned Sukey.

Kael glanced at a long, brown shape swimming toward him. He tried to run through the water, but his legs felt as heavy as rock.

Hands reached out to him.

Kael grabbed hold of them and leaped into the safety of the boat as the snake struck out.

Brota poked his nose over the side of the boat and jerked back as the snake lifted its head and struck the empty air.

"That is the largest snake I have ever seen," gasped Kael.

"They are all about that size," said Sukey, matter-of-factly.

“Let me try to move the boat,” said Gonter.

Sukey handed him the pole, and Gonter pushed the boat ahead.

Kael studied the area. Water stretched as far as the eye could see. Still, it looked like grassy land. Tall reeds waved in the wind and rippled the surface of the water. Long-legged white birds waded in the shallow water or perched in the low-growing trees.

"I see plenty of birds. What animals are here?" Kael asked Sukey.

"Large cat creatures with sharp claws, called Swipers. They sometimes stalk our people."

Sukey wrinkled his nose. "Growlers scare me the most."

Kael felt faint. "You have Growlers?"

Sukey nodded. "Big, black ones."

A shiver crossed Kael's shoulders. He touched the bear claw necklace he wore around his neck. He could not forget his fear of Growlers.

"See!" said Maida. "Homes."

A settlement lay in front of them on a mound of land that rose above the water.

"There is my brother, Mikko." Sukey pointed to a group of boys playing at the edge of the mound. "He is the one in the middle."

A tall, thin boy glanced over at them. "You are in trouble, Sukey."

Sukey's smile evaporated. He took the pole from Gonter. "They will be wondering who you are and where I have been."

The group of boys waded into the water to meet the boat. Sukey's brother reached up, snatched Sukey by the hair, and pulled him into the water.

Mikko laughed as Sukey tried to catch his

breath. "Where have you been, baby brother?"

Sukey gasped for air.

Brota leaned out of the boat and growled.

Mikko's eyes widened. His grip on Sukey loosened. "A wolf!"

Sukey gave his brother a smug look. "He will not hurt you. See?" He held out his hand and grinned when Brota nosed it.

Gonter sat in the boat at Brota's side, eye to eye with Mikko. "I am Gonter. My friends and I have come from the Land of the Whispering Trees."

"What are you doing with my brother?" Mikko asked. "Why is a girl with you?"

Maida's hands fisted on her hips. She remained silent.

"We have chosen to travel together. I am searching for my family," Kael explained.

“We also are exploring the world to learn things for our clans,” said Gonter.

"So, are you here to learn from us?" Mikko gave them a sly smile. "I can show you a thing or two."

Mikko’s friends chuckled.

Kael's spirits fell. Mikko was behaving like Damo.

Mikko clapped a hand on Kael's shoulder, his dark eyes sparkling. "I was only teasing you."

"He teases everyone all the time," said Sukey. He stepped away from his brother and ran up onto the shore shouting, "Mareki, I am home!"

Home. Kael stood a moment in the boat, looking at the peculiar structures on land. He had seen many places and many homes, but none like this.

CHAPTER SEVENTEEN

Kael climbed out of the boat and stood in the clear water. He glanced from side to side to make sure no snakes were nearby.

Safe on shore, he stared in amazement at the group of open-air structures that dotted the land.

"These are different," Gonter commented.

Kael nodded. Four poles were placed at the corners of each structure and held up a roof made of woven grass. There were no walls, only the roof and a dirt floor covered with grass. Several clumps of woven leather strips hung from the sloping beams of the roof.

"What are those?" Kael asked.

Mikko grinned. "Sleeping places. You do not get one unless you pass the challenge."

"Challenge?"

"He is only fooling," said a boy standing next

to Mikko. "Mikko always teases." He punched Mikko playfully.

An elderly woman approached them, hanging onto Sukey's arm. "Where are the visitors?" she asked, holding a hand in front of her.

Kael's surprise gave way to understanding when he realized she was staring at him with sightless eyes.

Maida stepped in front of the woman and took hold of her hand. "I am one of the visitors. My name is Maida, from the Land of Fire and Ice."

The old woman ran her fingers over Maida's face. "Ah, a beautiful child."

Maida's jaw dropped. Her eyes grew wide. "How do you know?"

The old woman patted her cheek. "My fingers tell me."

"My grandmother, Mareki, knows many things," said Sukey. "Magical things, too."

"*Life* is magical," Mareki said, smiling. "Now, where are the other visitors? Come, let me touch your face."

Kael and Gonter stood in front of Mareki

while she traced the lines of their faces with her fingers.

"Strong features," she announced in a tone of satisfaction. "Come, you must tell me about your travels."

Full of curiosity, a crowd gathered off to the side, watching them.

Mareki walked slowly, leaning on Sukey's arm.

Kael, Gonter, and Maida followed her.

At each step, Kael wondered how life would be if he could not see the lights in the sky, the flowers in the woods, and many other wonders.

As if she heard his thoughts, Mareki said, "I was born with sight. I lost it over a long period. This change has taught me to enjoy the memory of things past and to explore the possibilities of things to come into my mind."

"Grandmother says I can learn her ways," said Sukey. "She says it does not matter how little I am."

Mareki patted Sukey on the back. "Being wise has nothing to do with how big or how small a person is. Besides, Sukey, you have imagination."

Sukey grinned. "I am going to tell Mikko what you said."

Mareki shook her head. "The passage of time will take care of many things, child, including a brother who teases." She waved a hand about her. "Is the wolf I have heard about following us? Tell me about him."

Gonter drew to her side and told her about finding Brota as a baby.

They continued to walk toward a structure at the edge of the village circle.

Kael thought of his own stick and mud house in the cool forest, and entered Mareki's open-air home in the hot, humid marshlands.

Mareki's voice broke into his thoughts. "It is the different ways in which people live that help us to understand how alike we all are."

“Yes, I think so, too,” Kael said. The many people he met on his adventures lived in different houses, ate different foods, and played different games. They were much alike, too. Family, safety, water, and food were important to all of them.

"Ah," said Mareki, reaching out until her

hand settled on Kael's head. "We have a thinker in the group." She turned to the sound of Gonter's soft laughter. "The three of you are doing well traveling together."

The old woman lowered herself to the ground and patted a space beside her. Sukey sat next to her. Kael, Maida, and Gonter took seats opposite her and waited for her to speak.

"Good fortune brought you to us," Mareki said. “My people will learn from you, and you will learn from us. In the future, children will be a source of knowledge for all of us."

"A Night Flier helped us kill a Gouger," said Kael.

"Brota and I were trapped in a big hole...and we saw cave paintings...and lots of things," Gonter said.

“I saved them from bad hunters who wanted to kill the beast with the golden horn,” said Maida.

Mareki laughed. "So much to see and do. You came here from the Land of the Whispering Trees?"

"That is where they found me,

Grandmother," said Sukey.

"You visitors have done a good thing already," Mareki hugged Sukey to her. “You have brought my wonderful grandson back to me. It is through him that I ‘see’ many things."

"Will someone tell us about your sleeping places?" said Gonter.

"I will show you," cried Sukey. He jumped up and ran over to a mass of woven leather strips hanging from a beam inside the hut. He tugged on it, and it fell in a clump above the ground with a soft swish.

Kael watched as Sukey put one foot in the middle of it and sat down inside.

"It is much cooler for sleeping, up in the air like this, away from the bugs and snakes on the ground," Sukey said.

"Can I try it?" Kael asked.

Sukey got out, and Kael sat on the edge of it, dangling his feet.

“Like this?” He swung his legs around. The hammock flipped. And Kael landed on the ground with a soft grunt.

"You have to stay in the center," said Sukey,

"or it will flip over, then tumble you out."

"I want to try again." Kael got to his feet and inspected the sleeping place, trying to figure out where the center was.

Mikko approached and burst out laughing. "You fell out? I told you there was a challenge to it." He turned to his brother. "Mother wants to see you. Father, too. You cannot hide here with Grandmother forever."

Sukey softly kicked a foot in the dirt.

"Everything will be all right, little one," said Mareki. "Mikko is right. It is time to sit down and talk with them about what you have done. They were worried about you. Mikko, you entertain our guests while he is gone."

"Follow me down to the water," said Mikko. "We are playing a game."

Maida trailed the boys, wondering how girls lived in this clan. In some clans, girls were not allowed to play with the boys. They had to help their mothers with cooking and caring for the smallest children.

A group of young people, boys and girls,

were playing at the water's edge. They tossed a small round object back and forth.

Maida grinned. The small woven grass ball flew her way.

She caught it easily.

Everyone rushed toward her. Not knowing how the game was played, Maida turned and ran as fast as she could.

"You can stop now," puffed Mikko, catching up to her. "You won the point."

Maida turned around and gave him a smile.

Mikko grinned. "You are fast."

“Faster than you,” she said, and took off once more, leaving Mikko far behind.

They played the racing game until everyone was too tired to continue.

Kael sat with the others who formed a circle beneath a group of trees.

"Where are you from?" a girl asked.

“The Clan of the Forest. At least I was. We were raided. I am trying to find my mother and sister. They were taken captive.”

The girl nodded with sympathy. “I am sorry.”

Kael remained quiet. If he said anything more, tears might come.

Gonter told of meeting Kael and their trip to the Man of the Mountain.

Maida spoke about the hunters who had tried to kill them and how the three of them had saved the beast with the golden horn.

Sukey slipped into the circle and sat next to Kael.

Kael, Gonter, and Maida answered questions patiently, and then Gonter took out his sling and held it up.

"This is what I use to hunt," he said. "All three of us have learned to use a sling like this."

The young boys in the group pressed forward eagerly.

“See that tree over there? I will hit it with this.” Gonter loaded his sling with a heavy shell and whirled it over his head in a circle. He halted his twirling, and the shell spun out and flew toward a tree trunk.

Whap! It landed against the hard surface with a shattering sound.

Cheers erupted from the crowd gathering

and grew louder as Kael and Maida added their shell marks to the trunk of the tree.

"Will you show us how to make one?" Mikko's face shone with excitement.

"Sure," said Gonter, "if you show us the trick of your sleeping places."

Mikko laughed. "All right."

A man wearing a white feather in his dark hair stepped forward from the gathering. "I am Tomar, chief of the Clan of Rippling Waters. I saw what you did with your sling. I welcome you and your ideas to our clan."

"I found them," said Sukey proudly.

Tomar's brows shot up. He waggled a finger at Sukey. "You left our camp without telling your parents. You are one of us. Do not forget it." His voice softened. "We are glad you are back among your own people."

Sukey smiled. "I am not going to run away again. I promise."

Mikko placed a kind hand on Sukey's shoulder. "I will see that he does not."

The chief grunted softly and turned to Gonter. "You will get your wish. I will tell the women to show you how to make a sleeping place and how to use it. In return, you will show my hunters how to use your sling."

Gonter grinned.

A woman stepped forward. "I am Omah, the mother of Sukey and Mikko, and our new child, Neeno. Welcome to our home."

She led them to a structure nearby.

There, Omah showed them how sleeping places were made. Kael watched closely as she demonstrated how leather strips were knotted together, row after row, until a large rectangle was complete. Next, she showed them how she looped a braid of leather at each end, tying the strips together in a bunch. Then she took the extra length of braided leather at each end and showed them how to hang the hammock-like leather from the beams of the roof.

"How do we get into it without tipping over? Kael tried and could not make it work," said Gonter.

Omah moved the hammock until it was centered behind Gonter.

"If you do not get right in the center, it will

tumble you out," she explained.

Gonter backed up into the sleeping place and sat, careful to place himself in the center. Slowly, carefully, he swiveled around until his whole body was safely inside.

"I did it!" Gonter said.

"Not for long," grinned Mikko. He flipped the sleeping place over, tossing Gonter back on the ground.

"Mikko..." his mother warned.

"You are always teasing," complained Sukey. He offered a hand to Gonter.

Gonter got to his feet, shaking his head. Mikko's teasing was tiresome.

A tall, muscular man entered the home. Kael knew it was Mikko's father because they looked alike.

"Mikko's teasing again," said Sukey.

"Rotumi, these are our visitors," said Omah, ignoring the scowls between the two brothers. "I have invited them to share food and to sleep here."

Rotumi lifted his hand, his palm out in a gesture of greeting. "Welcome to our home."

He sat down on a log and waved them over. “Thank you for helping Sukey. He has learned a valuable lesson. Knowing when to travel and when to stay home is important." He touched Sukey’s bowed head.

Sukey lifted his face and turned to his father. "I will not run away again."

"There's no reason to do so," his father said gently. "A baby sister is fortunate for our family. And a big brother who teases is not unusual."

Sukey nodded. "I know, but now I want to go out in the world like Kael, Gonter, and Maida."

Rotumi smiled indulgently. "Perhaps you will."

After the fish stew had been eaten, Sukey jumped to his feet. “Come. It is story time. Grandmother tells good stories.”

Mikko and Sukey led them to the circle of young people seated in the center of the village. Even Brota was given a place next to Gonter.

The chief led Mareki into the middle of the circle, where she settled on the ground.

Silence fell.

"Today, we welcome three visitors and their

pet to our clan," she said. "They come from afar, so I will tell this story for them."

"Make it a Sneek story!" Sukey called out.

"So shall it be," said Mareki, smiling.

The children stirred restlessly, then settled down.

"Sneek was a lonely snake, not because he was the biggest, ugliest snake in the Place of Rippling Waters, but because he was the most dangerous. The minute he saw anyone pouting, he would make his purple body grow bigger and crush them. Some said he was unpleasant because he had an upset stomach; others said he was born that way. Whatever the reason, children learned to stay out of Sneek's way, especially if they were cranky.

"One day a little boy... We will call him Sukey..."

A loud gasp broke out in the group.

"It is only a story," said Sukey, though his wide eyes shimmered with fear.

Mareki continued. "One day, this little boy called Sukey decided to challenge his strength. You see, other children called him names and told him he was too small and too weak to go hunting with them. Sukey could not tolerate being teased. He knew if he could win a battle with Sneek, everyone would respect him. One sunrise, he poled his boat through the marsh, looking for that horrible, ugly, disagreeable creature. He whined and cried and waited. No Sneek. When he was about to give up finding him, a flash of purple caught him and began squeezing, squeezing, squeezing..."

Beside Kael, Sukey's breath caught.

"There he was," Mareki continued, "having his last breath being squeezed from his body by Sneek. Sukey barely had the strength to wiggle his fingers. He forced himself to do it. He moved one finger and another and another against Sneek's long, slinky body—up and down, with a poke here and a poke there."

The crowd of children held their breaths.

Mareki spoke. "Sneek's body began to twitch. A giggle broke out from him. Then, another. Finally, Sneek let out a small laugh that expanded into loud laughter. Sneek was laughing so hard he did not even try to stop

Sukey from wiggling free. Poor Sneek. Once he started laughing, he could not stop."

She smiled. "He laughed when Sukey got in the boat. He laughed as he followed Sukey through the water. He even laughed when Sukey showed the other children what to do if Sneek ever acted disagreeable again."

Mareki turned to the circle of children as if she could see them. "Sukey became a hero, of course. Not because he tamed the horrible old snake, but because he tried something different to solve a problem. He used his imagination. So, the next time things seem impossible, try to discover a new way to make them better."

Mareki clapped her hands. "Now it is time to go to your homes." She sat quietly while the children scattered in all directions to return to their open-air houses.

Sukey seemed to grow in stature as he led Kael and the others back to his home. "That was a good story. Grandmother says I have her gift of storytelling."

Mikko gave Sukey a little push. "It was not really about you. It was a story. Remember?"

Sukey playfully punched his brother's arm. Sukey was little, but like Gader, he had spunk.

Later, Kael lay in his sleeping place, looking up at the grass roof, listening to the sound of rain pounding on it. A warm feeling filled him. Here, he was safe and comfortable.

For once, he did not feel like he had to stay on alert for danger. He gave a sigh of contentment and drifted off to sleep, wishing things would always stay this peaceful.

CHAPTER EIGHTEEN

The sun rose, brightening the gray sky. Kael stretched, careful not to move too fast in his unusual sleeping place. A breeze blew across the space, cooling his skin. Quietly, he jumped down to the ground. Everyone else appeared to be asleep.

Brota stirred and followed Kael to Mareki's home. Many questions had filled his mind. He thought if he could get her attention alone, she might answer them. She seemed as wise as Ronoldo, the wise man in his clan.

When he arrived at her open-air structure, he was surprised to see Sukey sitting outside.

"What are you doing here?" Kael asked.

Sukey smiled. "I come here every sunrise to help Grandmother. In return, she is teaching me many useful things."

At Mareki's call, Sukey jumped to his feet.

"My grandmother needs my help. I will see you when I return."

Kael returned to the family's home to find everyone awake. Omah smiled at him and went back to stirring a mixture of bird eggs and herbs over a fire. She served him some in a wooden bowl. He ate it and wondered how the taste of the Big Water could be in his food. Puzzled, he took another swallow.

Omah smiled at him. "Have you never had water crystals?"

"What are they?" asked Kael.

"I will show you after we finish eating," said Omah.

After they had eaten every bite of food, Omah led Kael, Gonter, and Maida to a clear area of land off to the side of the village. Here, large leaves, like those found in the Land of the Whispering Trees, were spread on the ground. A thin coating of water covered some. Tiny white crystals lay atop others.

"These are the water crystals?" Maida leaned over to study them.

"Taste them," said Omah. "We use them to

flavor our meat and fish dishes."

Maida put a few crystals on her tongue. Her lips puckered.

"Do you like them?" Omah asked.

Maida smacked her lips and nodded. "Yes, now I am thirsty."

Omah chuckled. "Here in the hot lands, it is important to drink water. Water crystals remind us to do so."

Kael and Gonter tasted them, too.

Mikko dashed over to them. "Will the three of you show us how to use your slings now? Everyone is waiting."

Kael, Gonter, and Maida joined the men and boys who had gathered in the central circle of the village.

Gonter held up his sling so everyone could see how it was made. Then, he handed it to the chief.

Chief Tomar studied it and called to the women to come and look. "See how the strip of leather is cut out of one piece? We need to make some like it."

"I have cured skin I am willing to share,"

Omah announced. She left in a hurry, followed by several women.

"Once we show you how to use it, you can practice with ours," Gonter said.

Gonter demonstrated how to load the sling. Then he twirled it over his head, around and around, stopping suddenly. “You need to stop twirling at the right moment so the shell will fly out and go straight.”

He handed his sling to Mikko. “You try it.”

Kael grinned, wondering what kind of teasing would follow Mikko’s try. Mikko did well with the sling, surprising him.

Men and boys lined up behind Mikko, eager to try this new weapon.

"This is interesting," said Chief Tomar, observing them. "We can use such a thing to hunt our flying birds."

“Can I try?” asked Sukey.

“Not now, Sukey,” said Rotumi. “Let the bigger boys get used to it first.”

Sukey kicked at the sand with a bare toe. Watching him, Kael suspected Mareki’s Sneek story was really about Sukey, but he could not spend much time with the little boy. He was too busy helping the hunters get used to the sling.

Later, when it came time to settle down in darkness, Kael climbed into his unique sleeping place. A soft breeze cooled his skin and rocked the hammock. He was becoming used to this new way of sleeping.

Rays of sunshine broke through the darkness.

Kael rubbed his eyes and squinted in the early light, then noticed Sukey, standing nearby.

"I am going to my grandmother's house," Sukey whispered. "Do you want to come with me?"

Kael nodded. He had the feeling that Mareki needed to talk to him.

When Kael and Sukey arrived at her home, Mareki was standing outside. Her face was lifted to the sky. She turned toward them. "You both are here?"

Surprise struck Kael. How did she already know he was coming to see her?

Sukey grinned at him. "Yes, Grandmother,

Kael and I have come. I dreamed you wanted me to bring him to you."

"Thank you. Our connection is strong," she said. "Lead me down to the water, so we can talk while I walk to keep my body strong."

They walked along the water's edge, a boy on each side of the old woman who observed so much with her mind.

"I have had a special dream," Mareki said. "I believe events will soon challenge each of you. Remember the story of Sneek. It may help you meet the challenges you will face."

Fear squeezed the breath from Kael as surely as if it were Sneek himself. His life was one challenge after another.

Mareki placed a knobby hand on Kael's shoulder. "It has been told to me. I do not know what, or where, or why. I want you to be ready."

A shiver crossed Kael's shoulders.

Rotumi agreed Mikko could show Kael, Gonter, and Maida one of the clan's favorite hunting places a short distance away.

"Me, too?" asked Sukey.

Rotumi nodded. “Yes. This time, you may go.”

Sukey’s shout of joy made them all smile, except for Mikko, who did not bother to hide his disappointment.

Kael climbed into the flat-bottomed boat Mikko held in place for him. Worry clawed at his stomach. If Mareki was right about her dream, something awful might happen on this journey. Yet he could not stay behind, nor did he want to. It was a rare opportunity to see and experience something new.

Uneasy, Kael settled on his knees in the center of the boat beside Maida and Sukey.

Gonter stood at one end, a pole in his hand. Brota sat at Gonter’s feet, looking as if he wanted to jump out at any moment.

Mikko climbed in and stood at the front of the boat, and accepted the pole Sukey handed him.

"Can you push the boat without falling in, Gonter?" Mikko teased.

“Of course,” said Gonter.

Kael smiled. Learning to pole in the soft

bottom of the water was almost as difficult as learning to use the sling.

With two people poling, the boat made steady progress through the shallow water. The sun rose higher in the sky and sparkled on the rippling waves.

Kael took a sip of water from his water sac. "How much farther?"

"We are close," said Mikko. "In my clan, it is an honor for a boy to be allowed to travel to hunting camps. It is a sign he is becoming a man."

"What do you hunt where we are going?" asked Gonter.

"Growlers, large cat-creatures, and a number of flying birds," replied Mikko.

"Do not forget the snakes," said Sukey. "We do not hunt them, but sometimes we have to fight them to survive."

“Snakes?” Maida made a face.

Mikko’s eyes lit with mischief. "Sneek might be out here. You never know."

"He is teasing," said Sukey, looking worried.

"Perhaps," said Mikko, grinning. "Perhaps, not."

Kael could not help laughing. He leaned against the side of the boat and let his fingers trail in the clear water. He kept an eye on the surface, making sure no snake came close.

Mikko pointed ahead. "Our camp is there, among the trees on that island."

Kael cupped a hand over his eyes and strained to see. The land was hilly and covered with trees and undergrowth.

They approached the shore. Sukey jumped over the side of the boat and tugged on it. Mikko and Gonter pushed with their poles, moving the boat closer to land.

Kael climbed out of the boat and waded to the shore. The shoreline consisted of sand as white as the snow in the Land of Fire and Ice. Kael smiled and wiggled his toes in its softness, then turned to help pull the boat way up on the sandy surface.

They unloaded their travel packs and furs. Sukey led them through the trees to a clearing where two open-air houses stood.

"Uh-oh," said Mikko. "It looks like a Growler has been here before us."

In one of the houses, everything looked normal. In the other, sleeping places hung in shreds, and long, deep scratch marks marred the poles of that building.

Kael's heart skipped a beat as he inspected the poles more closely. Gonter came up behind him and stared at the claw marks. "That Growler must be huge."

Kael felt sick. He had no wish to share a small island with the animal he feared most.

Mikko set down his gear. "Let's go to the spring for a swim. We will bring back fresh water. The water there has no water crystals; we can drink it."

Kael followed the others down a trail away from the campsite. He heard the bubbling spring before they came upon it.

Gonter grinned. "Beat you!"

Kael laughed and chased after him.

Both boys jumped into the clear water at the same time, splashing Brota, who howled in surprise. His howls turned sad as Maida, Sukey, and Mikko joined Kael and Gonter in the water, leaving Brota alone on the bank.

Kael floated on his back. The cool water felt cool and refreshing after the heat of the sun beating down on his bare back.

A while later, they returned to the camp and worked together to get things organized.

Mikko took down the shredded sleeping places so the women of the village could repair them.

Sukey got a fire going.

Kael and Gonter scraped the feathers off a couple of birds they had shot down with their slings.

Maida picked meat off the bones for their meal, throwing the scraps of meat into a leather cooking sac filled with water and herbs to make soup. As she unrolled the leaves around the mushy mixture of grain and berries Mikko's mother had made for them, they settled down to share this meal together.

CHAPTER NINETEEN

"Wake up!" shouted Sukey. "Mikko's gone! In my dream, my Grandmother told me he is in trouble. We have to go to him."

Maida jumped down from her hammock. "Where would he go?"

Kael stared at Mikko's empty sleeping place. Was this the challenge Mareki had warned him about?

Tears rolled down Sukey's cheeks. "Mikko is in trouble. I know it. I had a bad dream about him. We must find him. Hurry!"

Kael grabbed his spear and followed Sukey and Maida. Behind him, Brota trotted at Gonter's side, nose to the ground.

The sight of Mikko lying on the path brought them to a halt.

"Do not move him," Sukey cried out. He knelt beside his brother and studied the red spot on his leg. “Snake bite. Grandmother told me that when such a thing happens, we have to get the poison out. She also said to keep him still, so it will not spread."

Maida knelt beside Mikko and touched his forehead. "His skin is hot to the touch."

Kael studied the area to make certain the snake was not nearby.

“Hand me a knife,” said Sukey, sounding grown-up. “I need to drain it like Grandmother showed me."

Gonter handed him a knife and stood nearby.

"Hold him still," said Sukey.

The three of them held onto Mikko’s arms and legs.

With one slash, then two, making an X, Sukey cut the flesh surrounding the bite. Then he squeezed the poison out and used Gonter’s water sac to pour clean water over the wound to rinse it. “We need to find leaves to cover it.”

“Be certain the venom is all out,” warned Kael.

Sukey nodded. "I think I have it all."

Maida dripped water from the water sac onto

the hem of her leather dress. She wiped the cool leather across Mikko's forehead.

"We cannot move him. We need to bring my grandmother here," Sukey said. "She will cure Mikko."

"I will go with you," said Gonter. "I am the best with the boat."

"Then, I will stay with Maida and help her take care of Mikko," said Kael.

"Keep Brota with you," said Gonter. He and Sukey ran to the boat.

Kael gripped his spear and held onto the leather strip around Brota's neck to keep him from following.

Maida went to the campsite and returned with her water sac and skins. She soaked the skins with water and placed them on Mikko's body. She rinsed leaves and covered the wound.

Maida gave Kael a worried look. Tears shone in her eyes. "He might not survive."

His hand on his spear, Kael sat beside Mikko, watching helplessly as Mikko struggled to breathe. Brota lay next to Kael, keeping watch in his way.

Kael's head began to nod sleepily. He fought to keep his eyes open. Mareki's warning reminded him to stay alert.

Maida lay on the ground, sleeping next to Mikko. A knife lay beside her hand.

Sometime later, Kael's eyes closed. His head slumped on his chest.

Brota's growling awoke Kael. Heart pounding, Kael glanced around. He saw nothing. Brota continued to growl. His fur formed a ridge along the center of his back.

Kael grabbed his spear and scrambled to his feet.

Maida stirred and sat up. Her eyes widened, and she screamed. "Kael, behind you!"

Kael whipped around.

A huge Growler broke through the undergrowth and stopped, staring at them. With a frightening roar, it rose up on its hind legs.

Brota lunged forward, attacking the beast, drawing blood with a bite to one of the Growler's hind legs. Letting out an ear-splitting roar, the bear swiped at Brota with broad, sharp claws.

Brota yelped and dropped to the ground.

"No-o-o-o!" Kael aimed at the Growler with his spear. The Growler's roars almost blocked the words in Kael's head.

"Remember what I taught you."

Kael faced the enemy he feared most. Wounded by Brota, the Growler would fight to the end. Like his father, Kael had somehow been chosen to fight this beast to save others.

"Be calm, aim true, keep steady."

Kael knew he had one chance to kill the Growler. He had to get close enough to pierce its heart.

The Growler rushed forward. Its hot breath brushed Kael's face. The dirty smell of its fur filled Kael's nose.

"Now!" His father's word came to Kael.

Kael thrust the spear into the Growler's body with all his might.

The Growler roared and jerked back. The spear hung from its chest.

A claw swung at Kael, brushed his cheek, and knocked him to his knees. Kael gasped with pain and drew in a shaky breath. Blood dripped onto the ground.

"Stay back, Kael!" screamed Maida. She twirled her sling and let a stone fly. The stone bounced off the beast's head and fell to the ground.

The Growler roared and staggered on its hind legs, striking out.

"The knife! Give it to me," shouted Kael, crouching on the ground.

Maida tossed it to Kael.

"Help me," Kael whispered to the night wind and threw the knife.

The blade entered the beast's chest, finding its heart.

The Growler fell forward, landing on the sharp point of the spear still stuck in its chest.

A heavy paw and sharp claws caught Kael when he tried to scramble away. His breath left him as the weight of the Growler pressed him into the ground.

The light dimmed as Kael lost his vision.

CHAPTER TWENTY

"Maida, what happened?" Gonter cried, his eyes wide at the sight before him. “We returned as fast as we could.”

Tears ran down Maida’s cheeks. "Help me!" she cried. She tugged on the dead Growler. "Kael is under the Growler. He is injured."

Sukey’s father, Rotumi, ran to Maida's side. Chief Tomar and Sukey appeared, walking on either side of Mareki.

“Help us!” said Maida.

Mareki knelt by Mikko.

The Chief and Rotumi helped Maida and Gonter roll the Growler off Kael. His face was covered in blood, and he lay still.

"Is he dead?" Maida’s voice caught in a sob. "He saved my life! Mikko's, too." Fresh tears streamed down her face.

Gonter knelt and shook Kael. "Wake up, Kael.”

Kael's eyes fluttered. His hand crept to the claw necklace he always wore in his father's memory. “I killed a Growler,” he gasped and closed his eyes.

"You are alive!" Maida clapped her hands and turned to the others. “He is alive!"

Chief Tomar and Rotumi checked his wounds and helped Kael sit up. “We will take care of your face. You are going to be all right.”

Gonter gave Kael an encouraging squeeze on the arm and turned away. “Brota! Oh, no.”

Brota whimpered, tried to rise to his feet, and fell back.

Gonter knelt beside the wolf he loved.

Brota gazed up at him mournfully.

Gonter stroked him on the head, studying the torn flesh and broken ribs that indicated trouble. He lifted Brota's head onto his lap unable to stop the sobs that escaped between his lips. Brota had been his pet since he and his father had found him in the woods, the lone survivor in a den of young ones. He could not die.

Gonter stroked Brota's head and turned to Mareki.

Sukey's grandmother was placing a leafy mixture on Mikko's leg, praying softly. Sukey stood watching her.

"Is Mikko going to be all right?" Gonter asked her from where he was sitting.

"I believe he will live," she said. "It is a good thing you knew enough not to move him. And good that Sukey drained the poison."

"I remembered what you once told me about snake bites," said Sukey.

Mareki smiled. "You have learned well, my child. You have saved your brother's life. You and Gonter found us and led us here. You have learned something else, I hope. Size makes no difference. Your heart is big. That is what matters."

She grasped Sukey's arm. "Lead me to Kael."

"W-what about Brota? Can you help him, too?" Gonter managed to ask.

Mareki rubbed Gonter's back. "We will care for him at home."

"He must get better!" cried Gonter. "I will not let him go!" Tears muffled his words.

"It is all right to cry," Mareki said softly.

"Seeing your pet badly hurt is not an easy thing."

Gonter held Brota close.

Brota's breath came out in sharp gasps. He looked up at Gonter and licked a finger, a sign of the love they shared. Then he closed his eyes.

Gonter's body shook with worried sobs.

Maida put an arm around him. "Mareki and others will do their best to save him." Silent tears of sympathy ran down her cheeks.

Gonter could only nod as he comforted the pet he loved.

Kael remained dazed as Rotumi and Chief Tomar led him to the spring, sat him down on its bank, and carefully washed the blood from his face.

"It is a good thing the bear's claw only grazed your skin. I think you will hold the mark for a long time," said Rotumi. "We will have Mareki work on it." He stood aside as Mareki approached, leaning on Sukey.

"Kael? I am here to help you," she said quietly. She knelt beside him, and her fingers traced the wound on his cheek. She turned to

Sukey. “Please bring me my bag of herbs. I will make something to put on the wound to protect it.”

“Is...Is Brota all right?” Kael asked. “The bear swiped at him.”

Kael’s breath caught in his throat when he saw Mareki’s sightless eyes water.

“It is bad, but we will keep him alive,” said Mareki. “Gonter is with him now.”

“I tried to save him.” Kael’s voice shook. The world could be a cruel place; he knew it well. He could not stop the tears that flowed down his wounded cheeks. He struggled to get to his feet. “I have to go to Gonter.”

Mareki gently pulled him back. “Give Gonter some time alone with Brota. He’s comforting the wolf and keeping him quiet.”

Kael sank down to the bank of the spring, wondering what would happen to the three of them without Brota. He had helped to protect them. He had made them laugh. He had earned a place in their hearts.

Mareki placed a mixture of herbs on Kael’s cheek. Then Sukey guided him to the open-air house and helped him into a hammock. "Grandmother said you are to rest, that it will help you heal."

Gonter appeared at Kael's side. Kael saw his tear-streaked face and patted him on the back.

"He is the best pet anyone could have." Gonter's voice cracked. "I cannot lose him."

"We will take him with us and perform a healing ceremony for him," said Mareki, joining them. She caught Gonter's hand. "We all want him to live."

Gonter nodded and silently turned away.

Kael awoke to darkness.

"Ah, he is awake," said Rotumi, walking over to Kael's hammock. "Come. It is time to eat. We have plenty of fresh meat."

Kael climbed out of the hammock and sat stiffly beside the fire. Every bone in his body ached from the struggle he had survived. His fingers traced the raw slash marks on his cheeks. He clutched his claw necklace, amazed he had won the battle with the Growler.

"You have become a man," said Chief Tomar,

nodding respectfully to Kael. "You have shown great bravery."

Kael remained silent. His gift of bravery had been tested many times, but never like this. He glanced at Gonter, lying in his sleeping place with his back to the group. He stared at the furs where Brota lay wounded. The wolf had shown as much bravery as he had. Perhaps more. His heart grew heavy at the thought of losing their four-legged guardian.

Mikko stirred on his furs and called out for water.

Sukey rushed to his brother's side. Mikko was fortunate to have survived.

"The difficulty of becoming a man," Mareki said quietly, breaking into his thoughts, "is in knowing the responsibility it brings. The wise man in your clan knew it was a good thing for you to travel the world. And Maida, with her kind heart, and Gonter, with his loyalty, are good companions."

Kael let Mareki's words fill his mind. It was a huge responsibility to travel the world, seeking not only his family, but truth and learning new things to share with others.

"You have been fortunate to have avoided tragedy for so long," said Mareki.

Kael nodded. The world was full of strange creatures and people who sometimes wished them harm. Ronoldo had warned him that he would be given many challenges.

Mareki called quietly to Gonter. "Come here, young man. I want to thank you for helping to save Mikko's life."

His face downcast, Gonter slid from his hammock to the ground and walked over to the group of them huddled together.

Mareki patted the ground next to her, and Gonter sat down. Mareki put an arm around him and drew him close. "It took a great deal of strength for you to come by boat to get me. It will take another kind of strength to go forward from here. I know how worried you are about Brota. Our hearts cry for you. You have things to do—learning about life and different places, so you can help clans everywhere. I believe Brota will heal in time, but he will be too injured to travel with you."

Kael gasped softly.

"H-h-ow can I leave Brota behind?" Gonter's eyes filled with fresh tears.

"Ah, child, you do not have to," said Mareki. "It has been spoken. He will remain here so we can love and take care of him. When you leave, his spirit will travel with you, in your heart."

Kael watched Gonter wipe his eyes and felt sympathy. Gonter knew it would be selfish of him to make the wolf suffer pain as he tried to keep up.

"Do you want to continue your travels from here instead of going back to our settlement?" Rotumi asked them.

Kael, Gonter, and Maida gazed at each other and nodded.

"All right then. At sunrise, Sukey and I will take you by boat to the place where the Land of Winding Woods begins," said Rotumi. "I have heard great forests lie beyond it."

Later, in the darkness, Kael lay awake as the others slept around him. Even Gonter had finally drawn the deep breaths of sleep. Images of the bear coming at him and the memory of its scent kept Kael from the comfort of sleep. His thoughts turned to his family. It had been such a long time since he had seen them.

In the gray light of a new sunrise, Sukey rose from his furs.

Kael joined him, and together, they walked down to the spring.

"Someday, I want to travel the world like you," said Sukey. "I might even take my brother along."

Kael smiled, though it hurt to do so.

They washed off in the spring and came back to join the others, eating a meal.

Rotumi and Chief Tomar helped them pack meat for their travels. The rest of the food intended for their hunting trip was handed over to Maida.

Then Kael, Maida, and Gonter each shared a private time with Brota.

Maida went first, whispering words of endearment and stroking the wolf she had grown to love.

Kael could not help the tears that filled his

eyes as he stroked Brota's head and quietly talked to him, thanking him for helping to keep him alive.

Finally, it was Gonter's turn.

Everyone else moved away to give him privacy. When he finally joined them, Kael understood the courage it took for Gonter to move on.

He, Gonter, and Maida lined up by the boat, waiting for Rotumi and Sukey to take them through the marshland.

Mikko hobbled over to them and gave each of them a weak hug. "Thank you," he said, serious now. I thought it would be funny to tease Maida with a green jumping creature from the pond. I was on my way to get one when the snake bit me. I have learned my lesson about teasing."

Sukey led Mareki to them and stepped aside while she laid a hand in blessing on each of their heads. "Travel well, my friends."

Chief Tomar addressed them. "I give each of you a white feather from the wading birds that mean so much to us. May you always remember us. The Clan of the Rippling Waters will keep

Brota alive and well, and we will tell the story of three travelers from different clans—travelers who helped us so much."

Kael held a white feather in his hand and lightly touched it to his wounded cheek. He had survived a battle with a Growler and would live to tell the tale. But he would carry in his mind the image of the wolf fighting to protect them. He lowered his head and could hear gentle words in his mind.

"Keep steady, Kael. Safe travels ahead."

# # # # #

For parents and teachers, here is a link to get a list of projects for classroom and home:

https://dl.bookfunnel.com/qtubymmu7g

Thank you for reading this book; I hope you enjoyed the story. If you did, please tell your friends or post a review on Amazon, Goodreads, Bookbub or any other links you might be familiar with. It's the kindest thing you can do for an author. Thank you so much! I love my readers!

Be sure and check out my other children's books:...

THE HIDDEN MOON – Twelve-year-old Jack Coughlin and his younger brother find a small wooden box that's supposed to hold magic. Instead of flying to the Space Center in Florida like Jack wants, the genie-like figure inside mistakenly sends them and a friend to outer space. On the eerie, hidden moon of Anron, where things are not what they seem and flying dragons carry them into battle, Jack must figure out a way to get them all home safely. An exciting adventure story for middle-grade boys and girls.

RETURN TO THE HIDDEN MOON – Jack wakes up to see the stone from Anron blinking on his bureau – three fast blinks, three slow, three fast. SOS! It can only mean one thing. Karna, Nidar and others on Anron need their help. Jack, Collin and Danny go back to outer space for another, even scarier adventure.

KERMIT GREENE'S WORLD - Kevin "Kermit" Greene's life isn't easy. The biggest bully in Middle School is demanding a fight between them. And being the quiet one in a loud, boisterous family, he's often overlooked.

His whole world changes when two tiny human-like creatures appear from another planet and tell him they are seeking a green hermit who has been talked about in their history as the Earth creature who will save their kingdom of Celabar from being destroyed. It takes them time to realize it's actually Kermit Greene they are looking for. Kermit agrees to go with them.

On Celabar, Kermit is the idol he has always wanted to be. But, to be worthy of the praise he receives, he must come up with a plan to get rid of the giant bird the Devastators are using to control people so they can steal the gold lying beneath Celabar's surface.

And the new Ancient Coming-of-Age Fantasy Series... When another clan invades Kael's clan, his mother sends him into the safety of the Forest. He emerges to find himself alone except for the wise man of his clan, who tells him he must travel the world to find his family and to learn about other clans so he can share knowledge with them. He warns him that he will meet strange creatures, even some who can talk, and there will be danger. Always danger. With no other choice, Kael sets out with his spear to explore his ancient world.

Kael's Quest -Book #1 in The Clan Chronicles series

The Walking River – Book #2 in The Clan Chronicles series

The Way Home – Book #3 in The Clan Chronicles series

ABOUT THE AUTHOR

J. S. (Judith) Keim is a ***USA Today*** **Best-Selling Author** of adult stories. She enjoyed her childhood and young-adult years in Elmira, New York, and now makes her home in Boise, Idaho, with her husband and their Dachshund, Wally, and other members of their family..

While she was growing up, books were always present - being read, ready to go back to the library, or about to be discovered. Information from the books was shared in conversation, giving everyone in the family a thirst for sharing ideas. Perhaps that is why she was drawn to the idea of writing stories early on.

As J. S. Keim, she writes middle-grade fantasy books for children. She particularly loves to write novels about characters who have interesting, fun, and exciting experiences with creatures both real and fantastical, and who learn to see the world in a different way.

ACKNOWLEDGEMENTS

Creating and producing a book requires the efforts of many people before it is sent out into the world. I'm grateful for the support of so many readers, family, and friends. I want to especially thank the women in my Wednesday morning writing group, Lynn, Peggy, Cate, Melanie, Niki, and Joanne, for their continued support and encouragement. The beautiful covers for the series are the creations of Elizabeth Mackey. Most of all, I want to thank my husband, Peter, for assisting me in the business and for being my other half in life.

Without all of you, this book might still be sitting on the shelf.

www.ingramcontent.com/pod-product-compliance
Lightning Source LLC
LaVergne TN
LVHW091120080826
845145LV00008B/1984

* 9 7 8 1 9 6 5 6 2 2 7 4 2 *